The Fiddler's Song

The Fiddler's Song

LaJoyce Martin

The Fiddler's Song

ISBN 1-57502-217-6

FOR INFORMATION:
LaJoyce Martin
202 South First Street
Morris, Oklahoma 74445

Printed in the USA by
Morris Publishing
3212 E. Hwy 30
Kearney, NE 68847
800-650-7888

Other Books by LaJoyce Martin

The Bent-Winged Series:

To Love a Bent-Winged Angel
Love's Mended Wings
Love's Golden Wings
When Love Filled the Gap
To Love a Runaway
A Single Worry
Two Scars Against One

Pioneer Romance:

The Wooden Heart
Heart-Shaped Pieces
Light in the Evening Time

Historical Romance:

So Swift the Storm
So Long the Night

Western:

The Other Side of Jordan
To Even the Score

Path of Promise:

The Broken Bow
Ordered Steps

Children's Short Stories:

Batteries For My Flashlight

Nonfiction:

Mother Eve's Garden Club
Heroes, Sheroes...and a few Zeroes

To
My Father-in-Law,
Frank Martin

TABLE OF CONTENTS

Chapter One

A New Generation

"Life never lets me *rest,* Sally," complained Martha Harris to her lastborn. "I thought when I got all my saplin's rooted in their own sod, my worries would pipe down. Then along comes a whole new generation o' frightful frets. . . My brain gets so tired it hangs 'tween my ears all limp and tuckered out."

"Let me guess," volleyed Sally. "It's Matilda."

"Yes, it's Tilly." Martha gave a tired sigh. "My Sarey's little Tilly."

"*Little?* She's twenty-two."

"She's still Sarey's baby."

"And that might be the problem," Sally countered. "Matilda needs to grow up. Besides, Sarah's children aren't yours to worry about. You raised yours, and she raised hers. Let Sarah stew over Matilda's woes."

"Now, Sally-girl----" Martha gave her a wounded you-don't-understand look. "You ain't never been a gran'ma. Bein' a Ma an' bein' a gran'ma all runs t'gether when you git as old an' mossy as me. You uneasy over yer gran'children same as you did over your own sons an' daughters."

"And then the great-grandkids climb on the worry wagon and the great-great-grand----"

"What scalds my feathers," interrupted Martha, shortening Sally's verbal nib, "is that yore Pa has been layin' a-*restin'* in yon graveyard fer seventeen long years an' I'm obliged to do both my worryin' an' his'n. That's a double whammy an' 'tain't fair." She jabbed an age-atrophied finger toward the front window through which the iron bridge spanning the Brazos River could be seen. Across the bridge lay the Brazos Point community cemetery where Henry Harris was buried.

"Mama, you know that if Papa was alive, he wouldn't spend his time with fretting. Papa didn't believe in dreads. Remember how he always said God's shoulders were broad enough to carry our loads? Papa never worried unless you worried him with your worrying."

"But he'd sure as eternity grieve o'er his own gran'daughter's backslidin'."

"I'm afraid you're judging Matilda, Mama."

"No, I ain't jedgin', Sally. The Bible plainsome sez ye shall know them by their fruits. An' I've seen some mighty rotten fruits on Tilly's limbs a-lately. When she came mincin' in here in that short-tailed dress an' them red shoes with th' toes a-missin', I knowed she had done listened to th' devil's whispers. Why, that dress was so skimpy you'd'a thought th' seamstress ran a-shy on material. Do you think my Ma would of let me out in public in sech a garb? Not on yer ferrotype! She'd'a sewed flour sacks on th' sleeves an' tail of it!"

"I hope you don't expect Sarah to----"

"Sarey lost th' game long ago. She let Tilly run bare-legged when she was in th' first primer. It galled me somethin' fierce t' see th' child without stockin's. It looked so--so *immodest*. But then, I'm old-fogeyed."

"Times do change, Mama. We crossed into the twentieth

century some time back. And I believe we've all profited by the change. Your son, William, drives a horseless. Your grandson, Michael, works at the railroad shops. And even yourself----" Sally inclined her head toward the telephone. "Alan and Chester can call you from Austin on the speaking horn."

Martha talked on as if Sally had said nothing. "Sarey hit a bad ball when she permissioned Tilly to go to work fer Mr. Jacob's son at the drugstore when she was fresh out o' school. I tried t' tell Sarey that warn't a good idee, but she wouldn't hear. Tilly wanted spending money. Tilly wanted new clothes. Tilly was bored a-sittin' home. An' at that drugstore is exactly where Tilly met that ungodly husband o' hers. That's where he flirted an' coaxed an' caught her: at her job. *He's* th' one who wants her t' dress an' act like a flapper! *He's* th' one who's strayin' her from her home larnin'! *He's*----"

"Mama, Matilda is grown now. She is no longer a child. She is responsible for her own actions. Sarah can't boss her around and neither can you. All either of you can do is pray and leave her to God's loving care."

Martha fished a napkin from her apron pocket to sop away the gush of tears. "Oh, I do that ever' day. She's on my tell-God list. When all my brood was younger, I recited 'em t' God in alphabetical order each mornin': Alan, Arthur, Chester, Dessie, Joseph, Matthew, Sally, Sarey, an' William. An' fer awhile, there was Effie, that precious little crippled-up angel that took off t' Heaven so's God could fix up her bent wings. An' our Robert that got kilt in th' horse runaway accident.

"Then came along all th' mates. Alan's Elise. Arthur's Lucy. Chester's Candice. Dessie's Nathan. Joseph's Amy. Matthew's Pauline. Your Jay. Sarey's Hank. An' William's Nellie. Now, with all them and their'n, there's more'n *forty,* an' my mind can't line 'em up in proper order any more. I jest clump 'em t'gether fer God an' let Him sort th' laundry an' git 'em clean or put 'em through th' wringer, whichever He needs to do.

"But now I'm separatin' out Tilly special, for I fear she's in danger o' th' lake o' fire." Her voice fractured. "I can't understand why Tilly would want t' stray. She's from sech a good family. Now if'n it had been Susan, William and Nellie's adopted, I might could figger it. We never knowed what was hid in Susan's ancestry. An' here Susan turns up with a pretty godliness an' Tilly don't!"

"If you'll think back, Mama, Sarah wasn't a paragon of perfection herself. Memory is a convenient sieve. You forget that she eloped with Hank when she had just caught up with sixteen birthdays. Mayhap she's reaping her harvest."

"But Sarey wasn't wicked; she was jest in turrible love with Hank. If'n she'd'a come to me an' asked--"

"No, you wouldn't have let Sarah marry Hank at sixteen."

"Well, mayhap not right *then*, but--"

"Matilda was old enough to wed with or without her mother's permission."

"Sarey's marriage was right an' good. Hank was a hard-workin', God-fearin' Christian boy with a fine head on his neck. I seen Sarey had made a wise choosin' 'fore th' first week fell off th' calendar. But with Tilly's match, it's not that way. Her man is a irresponsible fiddle player, besides bein' a hit-an'-miss shoe seller. Now is that any job for a real man?"

"He's working his way through college. He has to take whatever he can get. I think----"

Martha blocked her daughter's conversational path. "An' Sally, he plays that fiddle fer *dances*. All them ladies an' men out there *touchin' hands*! I think it's shameful; it makes me shudder.

"I know within reason that Sarey hoped on Tilly marryin' a

parson. Tilly could play th' pianola by ear twice as pert as most could play by note. An' she has a voice t' sing like a mockin'bird. She has wasted herself on that sinner, that's what she's done!"

"Be glad Matilda's husband treats her well."

"How can we be sure he always will, though? We know particularly nothin' of his beginnin', his raisin', ner his family. Tilly has never met ery one of them. Fact t' business, Sarey says he's keepin' his marriage a secret from his own Ma. Seems she's payin' on his education an' if'n she finds out he has wifed, she might stop his tuition. He sneaks off home ever now an' then an' pretends he's jest a schoolboy. Now is that deceitful in a man or what?"

"He only has half a year left to go, and then it won't matter."

"Can you imagine? Him an' Tilly have been married goin' on two years an' have that little boy a'ready--an' his Ma not even knowin' she has a gran'baby? Won't that rattle her shingles?"

"She'll be bound to love Matilda and Little Henry when she meets them. Matilda is likable, and Little Henry is a heart stealer. Wasn't it sweet of Matilda to name her son after Papa?" Sally left for the kitchen to check on the potato soup she was cooking for dinner, calling over her shoulder, "Everything will work out, Mama."

Sally meant to end the discussion and divert Martha's mind, but when she returned to the sitting room, she found that the subject was far from closed. It had become an obsession with Martha.

"I jest hope Tilly's husband don't ever take her with him to them dances where he fiddles."

"Likely, she stays home with Little Henry. She's a good mother."

"A good mother? I don't s'pose she's been t' church ery a time since she married. Bein' a good Ma means takin' one's children t' God's House."

"Matilda has her Bible, and she knows what is right. Give her time. All of us have had some foolish moments in our past that we'd like to forget--and in spite of our youthful folly, most of us have brought honor to the Harris name. Take me for an example. Have you forgotten that I ran away from home once? I'm none the worse for it; I learned a few good lessons. I'm settled and contented now. I have faith in Matilda that in time she will find her way back."

"But *you* got a good husband. Your Jay is a prince. That's the difference in you an' Tilly. Tilly didn't get a man like Jay. When two unites, they become one. I don't want Tilly harmonizin' with a wayward fiddler!"

"It's too late now; she's married to him. And besides, you've not given yourself a chance to know Matilda's husband. You haven't even met him."

"He's never showed his face here."

"Mayhap he's waiting for an invitation."

As usual, Sally's reasoning was an attempt to mollify Martha. But, as usual, it brought on another aggrieved tirade. Sally wondered why she bothered. Would she never learn that these mental wrestling matches were a waste of time?

"I ain't never gonna patty-cake with sin!"

"No one would ask you to do that, dear Mama." Sally's voice was resigned. "However, we can loathe sin without loathing the sinner. We must love a person whether or not we approve of his wrong deeds. As you have pointed out, we know nothing of the background of Matilda's husband. Perhaps he hasn't been exposed to Christian principles as Matilda has."

"But Tilly can't go along with evil in order to lead her husband to right. It won't work. An' there's Little Henry to consider. He's gotta be raised with salvation!"

Sally tried a new avenue. "I agree with you. Matilda never should have married an unbeliever. It's against the Bible. She has been taught better. But what is done is done, and we can't change it. Now we must try to make the best of the situation and hope for a happy ending. Please stop worrying before you make yourself ill again. Worrying can't help anything."

Martha had her way of making Sally feel guilty for scolding her. She used that tactic now. "Look at me, Sally. I'm old an' stove up. I ain't gonna be here much longer. My eyes won't let me piece quilts an' my hands won't plant a garden. What good am I to any o' you or to God?

"There ain't nuthin' left I *can* do but worry. Mayhap worryin' can't help anything, but I can't help worryin'! Like as not if'n I never worried, I'd never pray. With Marthy Harris, worryin' an' prayin' goes around holdin' hands."

CHAPTER TWO

The Interim

Matilda propped Little Henry in the wooden high chair that had been through Sarah's kids, Matthew's kids, Dessie's kids, and one of William's. Battered it was but still usable. The child banged his spoon on the tray and clamored for attention.

"Shush, Henry!" cautioned Matilda. "You'll have old Mrs. Neuse pounding on the door and telling us to quieten down again."

She stirred the watery stew, tasted it, and added more salt. In less than six months, Bert would be out of college and they could look for another place to live. Bert said they might relocate to Cowtown. Matilda's life had been spent in Bosque County, and the prospect of living sixty miles from Walnut Springs excited her. In a city there would be concerts and medicine shows and millinery shops. They wouldn't have to live in a cramped boardinghouse and eat tasteless cornpone. Bert would be less agitated and more attentive to her and his son. Here he was driven by his studies, his jobs, his lack of finances.

Then, too, she would get to meet Bert's family. The secrecy about their wedding would end. She didn't like living a lie.

Matilda did not doubt that Bert loved her, but their marriage hadn't had a fair shot. There had been rare moments of harmony, but for the most part, the past two years had been a bitter struggle.

Vultures of sickness and tension and unexpected expenses snapped up the crumbs of happiness.

She remembered the first time she laid eyes on Bert Conner. What dash and gallantry he had! He came into the drugstore with his friend, Pascal, for a bottle of ink. His eyes met hers and held as surely as if he had seized her hands in his own. For a brief span of time, the rest of the world was blotted out and they were alone, stranded on an island of churning emotions.

"Bert Conner! For Pete's sake, pick up your eyeballs and put them back in your head!" Pascal poked him in the ribs. "Haven't you ever seen a girl before?"

"Not like that one," Bert grinned, a slow, schoolboyish inanity that started with his mouth and ended with a wink of his eye, calling Matilda's attention to eyes that were the rich brown of syrup.

He stood a good six feet tall with wide shoulders tapering to a narrow waist. His was a bold handsomeness, heightened by dark copper hair, sun-bronzed features and an adorable cleft in his chin. *I could be his slave for a hundred years,* Matilda swooned.

He introduced himself and asked her name. "Matilda Gibson," he repeated. "You are a beautiful lady." He bowed. And that was the beginning of his many visits to the drugstore. It took but the brush of his hand against hers to cause Matilda's heart to shimmy.

Bert had a worldly wisdom, a careless attitude that appealed to Matilda. He charmed her as naturally as he breathed. She had been too serious, too hidebound to enjoy life. All she had known was church, the farm and family; she'd worked hard and played little. Bert convinced her that she should "lighten up."

Pascal was at Bert's heels like a shadow; the two were inseparable. Matilda didn't like Pascal, for she sensed something flawed in the fiber of his character. His eyes were restless. She wished that she and Bert could hold a conversation without Pascal smirking in the background.

That chance came--well, almost--when Bert asked Matilda to the school's holiday banquet. Pascal showed up there, too, and dogged their tracks, but they had an opportunity for a few words alone.

"Your green eyes and that beautiful russet hair have not only turned my head but my heart as well, Matilda," he said. He teased a lot, but she saw that he was not teasing. He liked her, perhaps was even beginning to love her.

Like a sled going downhill, the romance gained momentum from that night. Matilda went home from work each afternoon dreamy-eyed and distracted.

"I can't get married until I finish school, Matilda," Bert told her one day in the presence of Pascal. "I promised my mother that I would wait until I graduated to take a wife. That will be two more years. My mother is helping to finance my education, and it wouldn't be fair to her to take on more expenses."

"I can wait," Matilda said.

"I'll marry you now," piped up Pascal. "I didn't make any rash vows." Bert shot him a murderous look.

The waiting, as well as Pascal's insistence that he be the groom, grew more noisome each day. Both Bert and Matilda were miserable with each other's nearness and more miserable apart.

Finally, Bert ditched Pascal long enough to whisper to her. "We could get married and keep it a secret. Mother never comes here; I go home for a weekend once a month. I could keep going home as usual, and she'd be none the wiser. Then I'd present you to her as a surprise when she comes for my commencement."

The more Matilda thought about it, the better it sounded. A glad light played in her eyes. "I'm game if you are!"

"All of life is a game with me," he chortled. "I just need a partner."

"This is a proposal?"

"This is a proposal. Quickly, while Pascal has his back turned: Will you marry me?"

"While Pascal has his back turned, I will marry you, Bert Conner."

They both laughed.

"We will need to keep the ceremony quiet and simple. That way, there will be less chance of my mother finding out. We could just slip away somewhere to ourselves."

"Pascal won't tell?"

"I'll bribe Pascal, the rascal!"

The prospect of telling her grandmother about her wedding plans discomforted Matilda. She could not pinpoint the reason. Why should she crave Martha Harris' approval anyway? The old woman was two generations behind in her thinking and headed for the crypt. Yet Matilda coveted her blessings even as Jacob had desired Isaac's.

Finally, Matilda decided it would be better to tell her mother and let her mother relay the news just in case Martha Harris "hit the roof." She wanted no roadblocks to impede her journey to matrimony.

Sarah took Matilda's announcement with motherly fortitude. She asked a few key questions: Where did they plan to live? How did Bert purpose to support them? Did she know anything about his rearing?

"Bert has a room in Mrs. Neuse's boardinghouse near the school," Matilda answered the first question. "I'll move in with him there. The rent will not go up much." To the other questions, she replied, "I'll keep working at the drugstore, and Bert will find whatever part-time jobs he can. With two incomes, we'll manage. I don't know anything about his family, but it isn't his family I am marrying, it is Bert. And I love him."

"But, Matilda----"

"You loved Dad enough to run away with him," Matilda reminded and knew she had hit a nerve.

"I'd known him all my life!" was Sarah's feeble comeback. "We were neighbors."

"Grandma says you never really know a'body until you live with them," retaliated Matilda. "I'm old enough to know who I want--and I know I want Bert."

When Martha Harris learned of Matilda's plans, she asked to speak with her granddaughter. Trepidation visited Matilda's mind, but she kept the appointment.

"Matilda," her grandmother said without preamble, "you've been accused of bein' my pet, an' I'm speakin' t' you out o' concern. Life's a bumpy road if'n ye ain't hitched up proper. I want t' know about this man's salvation. How does he feel about God an' church an' payin' tithes?"

"I don't know, Grandma. We've never discussed it."

"You mean to tell me, Tilly, that you've been seein' this boy for all these weeks an' ain't never talked of *God*?"

Matilda reddened. "I suppose we'll work all that out when we're united. We'll have a whole lifetime."

"After th' I-do's are said, it'll be too late. Most ever'thing else can be compatibled, but when it comes to soul matters, there'll be troubles sure if'n one b'lieves an' th' other'n don't. How can two walk t'gether unless they be agreed? Best find out if'n he's a b'liever, Tilly, an' only if'n he is could I give my go-ahead."

Matilda felt shy about broaching the subjects of God and religion. Bert had never brought them up; he had not mentioned attending church at all. The only reason Matilda compelled herself to discuss it was because she promised her grandmother that she would. Now she wished she hadn't.

When she mentioned God, a silence fell over Bert and lasted longer than a silence should. "I'm not religious, Matilda," he said. "I have managed without God for this long and have done quite well on my own. I'm not saying there is no God, but if there is, I'm certainly not acquainted with Him. You are welcome to your own religion, but I will ask that you keep it to yourself. Please do not try to impose it on me. I will tell you ahead of time that trying to turn me into a church boy won't work."

Matilda was disappointed and a little hurt; some bell of warning rang in her head. Worship had played a vital role in her family. She couldn't conceive of a life without prayer, Bible study or church attendance. Even the parson said, though, that serving God was an individual affair. She would keep her own integrity, and Bert would eventually see what he was missing.

A simple recitation of vows bound them together, and Sarah gave Matilda the old slat and leather trunk as a wedding gift. Matilda was now Mrs. Bert Conner.

Unfortunately, things hadn't worked out as Matilda had planned. Bert's room was a drab place with built-in loneliness that amplified the hollow moaning of the wind. She was glad for her job to keep her occupied while he was away. A few weeks into the marriage, however, she became too ill to work, throwing their finances into a tailspin. She learned that a child was on the way.

She grew weary of Pascal, who came for supper almost every evening. He made a pest of himself with his raucous laughter and brown remarks. Matilda was in no mood to entertain.

Pascal seemed to hate all forms of work. When he sat down, he remained rooted. When he stood up, he floundered to the nearest supportive object against which he leaned until necessity goaded him. Matilda considered him lazy. She wearied of stepping around him. He could at least move his feet!

She and Bert had their first big argument over Pascal. Bert offered to give him a key to their apartment so that he could come and go as he pleased. Matilda raised a fierce objection and refused to budge. For one frightening moment, she thought it might be she who moved out and Pascal who stayed.

Matilda read her Bible and prayed, but she sorely missed going to church. She felt her soul growing lean, her spirit weakening. There was an emptiness that prompted an inner ache. When she tried to explain her feeling to Bert, he hooted. "It's your physical condition, of course, Matilda! Your body is making changes."

When Little Henry was born, Matilda thought her joy would be complete. She loved children, had looked forward to having her own. Bert was proud of his son, too, but with the additional financial burden, it became necessary for him to take more work, and he was gone a great deal of the time. With no money for extracurricular activities, Matilda was stuck in the small, cheerless room with her child.

Then a terrible realization seized her. She was responsible for this innocent baby's soul. If she did not take him to church, how would he come to know God? But go alone? Bert slept when he wasn't working or going to school. She could hardly ask that he walk with her to the services.

Bert's job. . . He sold shoes, but that didn't bring in enough to pay the rent. So he played the fiddle for square dances. Matilda wasn't happy with the arrangement, but Bert seemed to enjoy furnishing music for such occasions. He called it a "cake job." Bert's fiddling was in demand. His datebook was filled with performances.

Matilda soon learned that he was a multi-talented man. He had artistic talents as well. On their honeymoon (which consisted of a twenty-four hour stretch without Pascal), Bert sketched her picture in realistic detail. He entitled the portrait "My First Love." Matilda treasured the painting. She framed it under glass to preserve it. It helped keep her love for Bert alive.

She had suggested that Bert sketch Little Henry, but he had not found the time for that. He promised he would make her request his priority when he finished with his schooling. By then, Little Henry would be able to sit still for a longer period of time.

Matilda had never heard Bert play his fiddle. (If she had gone to a dance to hear him, her grandmother would have invoked the wrath of God on her for attending such an affair.) However, she got unsolicited reports of Bert's performances from Pascal, who vowed to "keep Bert in line."

She made it from one lonely night to the next by reminding herself that the present trial was only temporary. The other world, the starlit one where love was easy, would have to wait. Soon Bert's once-a-month trips to see his mother would be history. He would be independent and have a regular job. They would have proper food and a house of their own where she wouldn't have to spend her hours trying to keep her baby quiet. If the thoughts failed to reassure her, she repeated them to herself with more inflection of challenge.

Yes, everything would change before long. . . .

CHAPTER THREE

Interrupted Evening

Matilda looked forward to a rare evening with Bert. She waited eagerly for the familiar footsteps that still made her heart quicken. "Daddy will be home to play with his buddy tonight!" She chucked Little Henry under the chin.

The child caught the festive spirit and clapped his chubby hands together. With the last of her flour, Matilda made a cake to celebrate.

She hoped that Bert would be in a good mood because she had a disclosure to make--and she wanted the setting to be right. Her crisply starched apron hid a secret; there was another baby on the way. She was elated, and she hoped that Bert would share her enthusiasm. She hadn't been sick at all this time. By the time the new member arrived, they would be well established in their own happy world, a world apart from exhaustion, deprivation and separation.

Bert came in, all smiles. "I passed my calculus test!" he beamed. "Only three more months of this brain-killing stuff, and we'll be out of here. Mmmmmm! What do I smell?"

"A cake. We're celebrating. And with good reason." She envisioned lighting the stub of a candle on the oilcloth covered table and making her grand announcement.

"You've been a brave cookie, Matilda," Bert said a little awkwardly. "I haven't always been fair to you and Henry. Sometimes I think I should quit school and take whatever employment I can get."

"Don't think of it, Bert! You are too close to give up now. Whatever the sacrifice, whatever the cost, you *must* complete your education. Times are changing so quickly. Without a degree, the struggle to survive would go on forever. Promise me that whatever happens, you won't throw in the towel with the end of our hardships in sight!"

"I promise. And at least we have this one night to ourselves. Let's try to enjoy it. What can I do to help with supper?"

"Nothing. But I do have a small favor I'd like you to do for me *after* supper."

"What you ask is my task."

"I want you to play your fiddle just for me. I've never heard you play."

"My pleasure!"

"And I'll sing just for you. And then----"

"You--*sing?* Is this a forte you've been hiding?"

"I used to sing at church. Grandma Harris says I have a million dollar voice."

"Do you think we could sell it?" quipped Bert. "A million dollars would start us on the road to recovery."

"Actually, I hoped you might play for me while I sing."

"I'd be delighted to if I know the song."

"It's *Amazing Grace*."

"Sounds intriguing. But I don't even know a girl by the name of Grace. Could we change the title to *Amazing Matilda*?"

Matilda frowned; she didn't like Bert being sacrilegious. Shallow joking offended holiness; it was like touching the tenderest part of the eye with a grimy finger. Yet when she looked into his face, she realized that Bert meant no facetiousness. He was being quite candid. He had never heard the song.

"It's a gospel song, Bert. About the unmerited favor of God for wretched sinners. It tells about being lost and then found, of being blind and then seeing. It is my favorite hymn."

The tense silence that followed hung heavy in the air. "In that case," Bert finally said, "I guess I'll have to beg off. My fiddle has never played a church song, and I'm afraid it would be as stubborn about changing over as its owner. I'll be glad to do *Yankee Doodle* for you or *Comin' Through the Rye*."

Matilda squeezed back the tears that tried to bud behind her eyes. She drew a curtain of reserve about herself, battling hurt and resentment. In the department of soul matters, Bert had not softened at all. The evening wasn't starting off right.

She had turned to check the cake in the oven when a knock at the door brought Bert to his feet. "Pascal?" she asked, irritation influencing her voice.

"No," Bert answered. "Pascal went to Kemball Bend to buy a roadster."

"Where did Pascal get the money for a car?"

"Beats me." Bert bunched his shoulders. "That boy can talk the horns off a billy goat."

"But I don't----"

He opened the door, stepped outside and closed it behind him, shutting off her words. The gesture agitated Matilda the more. Couldn't a single evening pass without conflict?

When Bert came back inside, his expression was an odd mixture of apology and relief. "I have to work tonight, sweetie," he said.

"Work?"

"There's a big dance out at Chalk Mountain, and the fiddler they had scheduled was called out of town on an emergency. The host is desperate. He has offered to pay me double to fill in for the regular musician. It's a lucky break for us. I can't afford to turn it down. The deposit on my cap and gown is due next week."

"Oh, Bert! And here I'd planned----" Matilda couldn't dam up the river of tears.

He put his arm around her shoulders. "I know it is a disappointment to you, Matilda. But what else can I do? You've made me promise to finish my schooling, and the income from my fiddling is my only means of keeping that promise. If you say the word, I'll drop everything."

"No. No, Bert. It's just that. . . Oh, I'll tell you later."

He looked at her with a bothered expression. "Matilda, I don't want to leave you. Maybe you could go, too. I've never invited you to go along with me to play for a dance because I didn't think it was something you'd enjoy, but I think it might be good for you to get out of the house tonight. You could wear the dress you wore when we got married."

Can I squeeze into it? Matilda asked herself, then aloud, "Could I take Little Henry along?"

"No," Bert answered without hesitation. "Children aren't allowed at the big socials."

"Then I can't go."

"I will be paid well. We could give Mrs. Neuse two bits to watch him for us. She'll do anything for an extra quarter."

"He would be no problem. All she will have to do is put him to bed, and he'll sleep until we get home. I--I wouldn't have to dance, would I?"

"Oh, no. I'd sit you where you could watch me fiddle, but you'd be out of the way of the crowd. We would only be going there to do a job, not for the party. There's a big difference."

"I think I'll go, Bert. I don't think I can stand another night away from you. I have a little secret to whisper in your ear."

"I'll have my ear cleaned out and ready. Is the cake done?"

"Yes."

"We'll have to eat and run. Mr. Davis will be by at six o'clock. That's less than two hours from now, and neither of us is dressed."

"We can do it. I'll hurry and heat the flat iron to press your shirt, and I can iron my dress quickly as well." A strange, new excitement bubbled up in Matilda. Her mother would be appalled and Grandma Harris would faint if they knew her destination, but it would only be this once. Some probity demanded that she hear her husband play his fiddle in his own element. She would not partake of any "forbidden fruit," and no harm could come of the outing. Martha Harris and Sarah Gibson need never know that she had gone to the dance.

With the help of her corset, Matilda buttoned herself into the dark green gabardine with its white linen collar and cuffs. She felt her midriff straining against the gores and was glad that the dress-up occasion wasn't even a week later. When she let her hair down into a cascade of waves, Bert whistled. "I'll have to hide you, or I'll lose you," he teased.

Bert made the babysitting arrangement with Mrs. Neuse, and Matilda kissed her son goodbye. It was the first time she had left him. Nettles of motherly misgiving stung her conscience.

"It's gladsome I am to see you get that girlie out in the fresh air," the elderly lady said to Bert. "She stays cooped up too much. That ain't good for nobody. Now you two just take your time and enjoy the evening. Babies are adaptable, and I've cared for a'many. So don't worry about this one. He's in good, capable hands. My, but you two are a handsome couple tonight!"

"To be such a crotchety old soul, she can give a good send-off, can't she?" Bert's humorous whisper made Matilda's apprehension lighten as they made their way toward Mr. Davis' rig. "And all for the love of a quarter!"

Horse-cars, Model T's, and fancy surries lined the lap of the hillside at the ranch. It looked as though the whole country had turned out for this one dance.

Bert upended a log for Matilda to sit on in the large barn-converted-to-dance-floor. Then he gave her a quick kiss and left her. "Behave!" he called over his shoulder, dropping one eyelid in a slow wink.

She took her seat, wide-eyed with wonder. The brilliant skirts and animated familiarity of the women made her feel like a species from the archives. She didn't fit in this throng. They made her nervous. Martha Harris would have called them "floozies."

Then Bert started playing, and her eyes were riveted to the bow of his fiddle. It slid. It bounced. It seesawed. It looked as if Bert followed its movements with the bends and turns of his head, his arms, his shoulders. The bow seemed alive with a mind of its own. The fiddle was playing *him*. She was mesmerized, fascinated. This was her Bert, and she hadn't dreamed he had a talent this magnificent. No wonder he was in demand!

Her eyes traveled to the dancers, swishing, swirling and hopping. Their hands welded them together so that they swayed as one unit. Now and then, the men caught the ladies around the waist, lifting them from the floor. The frantic gyrations seemed to loose some demon of liberty that should be kept under lock and key.

Swing your partner do-si-do. Everything changed. The lady with the red ruffles now took the place of the one in blue cambric. Did nobody mind whose hands they held? Would she hold hands with anyone other than Bert? What if the lady's waist grasped by the short, stocky man belonged to the tall gentleman with the black bowtie? Perhaps her grandma's objections to dancing had rhyme and reason after all.

Bert paid no heed to the bodies flinging before him. Matilda was glad for that; some of the flying skirts revealed far too much. Even though he seemed immune to it, she would be glad when this part of his life would no longer be necessary. She was grateful to be with him tonight, delighted that he'd held her hand all the way here in Mr. Davis' buggy. In his strong hands, hers were lost and warmed. But she would be glad to get home and away from this unwholesome atmosphere.

When the music stopped for intermission, someone threw a coin at Bert's feet. That started a trend, and a whole barrage of coins followed along with boisterous laughter and clapping. The coins caught the light of the lanterns, creating a dance of their own. Matilda wasn't sure whether she liked the gesture or not. Her Bert wasn't an organ grinder!

Then she wondered: Was Bert ever humiliated by the charity of those for whom he fiddled? The nickels and dimes tossed at his shoes bought cornmeal and sorghum and soap. With her contemplation came a revelation. He was doing this for her and for Little Henry. Her love for him took on a new proportion.

He looked toward her and mopped his brow. She gave him an encouraging smile; the dance was half over. They'd make it through and go home with the money. She'd tell him how proud she was of him, how she loved him for the sacrifices he made for her and his child--and she'd whisper the good news in his ear on the way home.

During the final number of the evening, Matilda made her way to the ladies' privy. She wanted to be comfortable for the cozy ride home. It was a short walk from the dance barn to the outhouse and well lighted. The path was quiet and momentarily deserted. The sky, clear and enormous overhead, offered a sharp and unlimited visibility, displaying a spangle of stars in their pure brilliance. It was a perfect night, a night that gave no premonition of what was ahead for Matilda Conner.

On her way back to the safety of the barn, a man stepped from the side of the footpath, causing her to utter a small cry.

Chapter Four

The Ruse

"It's only me, Matilda." The voice was unmistakably Pascal's. "Listen. I just came from Mrs. Neuse's, and your little boy has become quite ill. She sent me for you."

"Oh!" Matilda's hand flew to her throat. "I'll go tell Bert."

"No, you mustn't disturb Bert. That's against the rules. He's in the middle of a tune, and he would be angry if you disrupted the party. He might not get his pay. Hosts are very sticky about that. I'll take you directly home then return to let Bert know where you went. With my new roadster, we can get there much faster than a buggy could."

"It won't take but a minute, Pascal. I'll leave word with someone." She looked around, but there was no one in sight.

"I'm afraid you don't understand, Matilda. There isn't time. Your son is very, very low."

Suddenly, a taste of fear filled Matilda's mouth, sending a shivering weakness through every joint of her body. "Is--is he dead?"

"He was still breathing when I left. But *hurry*!" He took her by the arm, gripping it too tightly, and maneuvered her to his automobile, which he had parked on the outskirts of the traffic so that he might accomplish a speedy getaway.

Matilda's mind grappled for some order in the confused rush. She was torn between duty and desire. Bert would want to know. No concert meant as much to him as his child did. Pay or no pay, he would drop the fiddle and run home if he knew Little Henry's life was in danger. What had happened? The baby had been perfectly well all day without a sniffle or sneeze. Had he choked on something? Mrs. Neuse had promised to take good care of him, and he should have been asleep long ago. That would preclude an accident.

"Was--was there an injury?"

"No, he just took sick sudden-like. Mrs. Neuse said that it is not uncommon in children as small as Little Henry." As Pascal talked, he drove with manic speed, taking the mountain curves on two wheels.

"Please slow down, Pascal, or we'll never reach town," implored Matilda, but her plea only served to goad Pascal on. He gripped the wheel and leaned forward with a devilish determination.

"I know what I'm doing," he said.

The dawning came slowly. Matilda smelled a sour odor. At first, she associated it with motor fuel. Then she realized that the fermented scent was that of hard liquor. Pascal had been drinking! A tiny chill pricked the skin along her arms.

"Stop this vehicle and let me out!" she demanded, trying to keep the quiver out of her voice. "I will *walk* home."

"You will *ride* home, dolly," hiccoughed Pascal. "But home is not where you suppose. Your home will be with *me* now." Only then did Matilda take note of the direction they were going. Walnut Springs lay behind them, growing more distant with each speed-whipped moment.

"Where are you taking me, Pascal?" She assumed a deceptive calmness. "My baby is ill, and I haven't time for a joyride or for you to show off your new car!"

"You're a real dullard, dolly, if you haven't figured out what is going on. Your baby isn't ill at all. That story was a spoof to get you away from Bert. I've been waiting for this chance for two years.

"The fact is you belonged to me from the start. I saw you first in the drugstore and dibbed on you, but Bert stole you away from me. Just because he is a year older doesn't give him a right to run over me.

"I thought if I'd bide my time, he'd get tired of you and ditch you. I didn't bank on him keeping you permanent. I'm tired of waiting. . . ."

"Pascal! You have been drinking!"

"What's new? I took up drinking because I couldn't have you. Now I'll have you, and Berty can take his bottle for awhile. See?"

"Bert won't drink."

"Want to gamble on it?"

All of Matilda's senses clawed for a solution to her present dilemma. She had no precedent to call upon in dealing with a besotted brain. No one in her family had ever been under the influence of alcohol.

What would be her best recourse? With the passing of time, did a drinker's thinking become clearer or more clouded? Would Pascal be more capable or less capable of controlling the vehicle? Would he slow down or fly on even faster?

Over the interminable minutes, they sizzled through two small communities, over bumpy railroad tracks and across narrow wooden bridges. The car bucked and rattled, sometimes tossing her about with pitiless abandon.

She feared for her unborn baby, but there was no need to

mention her plight to Pascal. He would take a perverse pleasure in destroying Bert's posterity. When a tire slipped off the road, he fought with the steering wheel while the car spun and skidded. Matilda's outcry kept growing and swelling until it became a long, thin screech.

The car arighted itself.

"Be calm, dolly," Pascal advised. "I can drive better drunk than most people can when they're cold sober. You've never ridden in a car, have you?"

Matilda's teeth chattered. Her long fingers twined and untwined. "Y-y-yes. My Uncle William has a car. He lives in Cleburne. I-i-is that where we're going?"

"Naw. We're going the opposite direction. To Garden City. Some people call the place Temple. That's where you and I will live. It's a nice little railroad town. Ever heard of it?"

"N-n-no."

"I'll teach you to drive this machine when we get set up. We'll take the top of this jitney down and let that pretty hair of yours play in the wind. I won't keep you holed up in a boarding-house like Bert did. I'll show you off."

If I could get to the lever, Matilda thought, *I'd set the brake.* But the lever was on the left side of Pascal. She'd have to sit on his lap to reach it.

"You're looking beautiful tonight. All duded up." Pascal took his eyes off the road and gave her his attention. "That's your wedding dress, isn't it?"

What about the door handle? She needed to find it so that when or if Pascal slowed down, she could jump out.

"I bought this car for you." Pascal reached under the seat, pulled out a bottle and took a long draw.

"Pascal, please don't drink any more."

"The more I drink, the better I can drive and the more I love you. I want to get you home sh-shafely, dolly. Sh-shee?"

A frantic urgency tightened Matilda's chest. She hoped they didn't meet another car; Pascal was wobbling all over the road. She had to do something. And quickly! *Dear God,* she prayed under her breath, *get me out of this mess.*

What would Bert think when he found her gone? He would be beside himself! And worst of all, he wouldn't know how to pray, how to lean on God. *If two of you shall agree,* the Bible said, but she was on her own.

How could she get back to the Springs, back home? She hadn't a penny for carfare--or anything else. She needed to return in time to prepare Bert's breakfast. Little Henry must not awaken and find her gone.

What time was it now? It seemed an eternity since they left the ranch.

"H-how far is it to Garden City?" she asked, her voice an octave too high.

"Depends on how fasht we go, dolly. Like thish, fasht, an hour or sho."

"Then we shouldn't be far away."

"You're getting anxious, aren't you? I am, too, dolly."

"Where will we. . . stay?"

"That's a shecret." He laughed, an obnoxious, drunken guffaw. Then he helped himself to another gulp from the bottle.

His reflexes were getting slower. That could be good, or it could betoken a disastrous end. By the time they reached town, Matilda decided, he wouldn't have the wits to keep from wrecking the roadster. She watched for an opportunity to make her exit.

I must be ready. She slid toward the door and grappled for the handle.

"Oh, no, you don't!" barked Pascal. "Don't think you'll bail out on me!" He grabbed for her, abandoning the wheel to its own devices.

The car careened and spun then straddled a ditch, its fender striking a fencepost. Matilda parted her lips to shout at Pascal, her stunned brain demanding a scream of rebuke. Yet she was unable to make a sound. The entire drama began and ended in a few seconds. Matilda's head bashed against the window, and she remembered no more.

Pascal, groggy and limber-limbed, was not injured. He looked at Matilda, crumpled into an inert heap, with chagrin. "Whatsh happened, dolly?" he asked, shaking her. When she did not rouse, he drew back in a belated spate of fright. "Are you *dead*? Wake up, and I promise I'll turn around and take you back to Bert. I will explain everything. I'll tell him it was all my fault. I had already decided to take you back anyway. Women are too much trouble." He checked her pulse, relieved to find a heartbeat.

Crawling from the car, he pushed it away from the post. The brisk night air, along with the shock of the accident, served to bring some clarity to his mind. "And will Bert be mad at me if I've hurt his Matilda!" he muttered. "He'll find me and beat me to pulpwood. He might even turn on me and have me locked in prison. . . ."

The more Pascal talked to himself, the more panicky he became. "Please don't do that, Bert," he begged as if Bert were standing over him with a bullwhip. "I'll see that Matilda doesn't die. I'll get her to help somewhere."

The moon hung high and bright overhead, silhouetting a farmhouse in the distance. He nosed the car out of the ditch and toward the dwelling. If there was a woman there, she would surely know what to do for a fainting girl. Matilda probably wasn't hurt;

she had likely passed out from sheer fright. Poor girl. She wasn't accustomed to cars. Cars could do crazy things to flighty females.

He parked in front of the house with the damaged fender out of sight and picked Matilda up in his unsteady arms. The dogs set up a bark, and the guineas squawked. He wished they would keep quiet. He'd rather annouce his own arrival.

When he was almost to the front door, he realized that he would have to make some explanation for Matilda's lack of consciousness. Oh, well, he'd invent something; no one could learn anything from what was left unsaid. He certainly didn't plan to be charged with kidnapping.

A lamp-toting farmer's wife appeared at the door in her flannel gown and nightcap. "Yes?" She held the lantern in front of her and peered out at him.

"Ma'am, I was coming home late from a brush arbor meeting, and I found this young lady knocked out beside the road. My headlamps picked up the white of her trimmings. I don't know who she is. I don't recall seeing her at the church service. I suspect she was in some sort of accident. She doesn't seem to be broken anywhere, but she's mighty sleepy. . . ."

The woman stepped back. "Bring her in and lay her on the davenport."

Pascal followed her instructions, careful to stay in the shadows out of the lamp's light.

"Nor does she seem to be bleeding anywhere," the woman said.

"She's all dressed up like she'd been somewhere special."

"I thought mayhap she was a neighbor, but I don't recognize her, either." The woman held the light over Matilda's face. "She doesn't belong to the Lennocks or the Jarvises or the Tortzes."

"I didn't know what else to do but bring her to the nearest

place."

"You did the right thing. I'll see after her. Someone will be by looking for her. You were awfully kind to stop and give aid. If it was my Dora, I'd hope a nice gentleman like yourself might happen along. I wonder what happened?"

"I'm thinking she went to sleep and fell out of the back of a wagon, and her folks won't miss her until they get where they're headed. Like as not, the girl will remember it all in the morning. Her family will be more than grateful to you for sheltering her until they call for her."

"The Bible says do unto others as we'd want to be done to. That's our Christian duty."

"Ma'am, my Christian duty is to get on to Belton to my bedridden and widowed mother lest she worry herself into an apoplexy. Are you sure that you don't mind my leaving her? Can I pay you for your trouble?"

"Oh, no, no! Off with you to your mother! I'll take her over to Garden City to Dr. White's hospital in the morning for a medical checkup. My name is Vinnie Campbell. And yours?"

"John. John Brown."

"Mr. Brown, I regret that I wasn't at the revival tonight myself. I trust you had a good service. Our cow, Sukey, wandered off, and by the time I found her and got her milked, it was too late to start out. Everyone would have been at the mourner's bench by the time I arrived. But I hope that I shall see you there tomorrow night."

The closer Pascal got to his car, the faster he ran.

Chapter Five

Missing

Out of the corner of his eye, Bert had seen Matilda leave the building and guessed the reason she stepped out. He was proud of her; she looked elegant in the dark emerald dress. It brought out the green in her eyes, the amber highlights in her long, silky hair. She was coping with the melee better than he had hoped, yet he would be glad when they could leave. He looked forward to holding her hand in his on the way home. And she'd said she had something she wanted to tell him.

Matilda was different from the skin-deep girls who whirled about the dance floor. That is what had attracted him to her. Her beauty went to the bone, needing no exterior advertisement. She didn't abuse her eyes with soot or her nails with garish color. He resolved when he married her not to push her into a world foreign to her nature.

He liked her like she was except for her overzealous attitude toward religion. It made him uncomfortable when she talked about God and church. He had to draw a line somewhere, and he had drawn that line this afternoon when she tried to con him into playing a religious song for her that he had never heard and didn't care to hear. He'd warned her before their marriage not to badger him. While this and a hundred more things circled through Bert's mind, he fiddled *Turkey in the Straw* without missing a note.

The dance ended. He held up his fiddle in one hand and the bow in the other, giving his usual grand finale curtsy. The rabble of dancers applauded, and it was over. But Matilda had not returned to her place on the improvised stool he had provided for her. Where could she be?

Bert lay the fiddle in its case and snapped the lid shut. Mr. Davis approached, smiling and with his hand extended. "A grand performance, Mr. Conner. You saved the day for us. I'm paying you more than I promised." He stuffed a roll of bills into Bert's pocket. "And when you are ready for transportation to town, I am at your service."

"I will find my wife and we'll go," Bert said. "We seldom leave our young son, and I'm sure Matilda is anxious to get back to him." He caught the handle of the fiddle case and stepped outside, expecting to find Matilda returning from the outhouse. She was nowhere in sight.

Ladies milled about. He stopped one of them. "Would you check the ladies' room and see if my wife is there, please?" he asked.

She pursed her lips and batted her lashes double-time, reveling in male attention. Her tawdry dress appeared to be falling off her shoulders. "Certainly, Mr. Conner." He didn't know why women tried so hard to be seductive; it was disgusting.

He waited impatiently, somewhat worried.

"No, she isn't there, sir. Is there anything else----?"

Bert walked away. Where would Matilda have gone? He circled the barn then went back inside to search among the dispersing crowd. Matilda had seemed to be feeling well. She'd sent him a cheery smile at intermission.

He hurried to Mr. Davis' carriage in case she had gone to

wait for him there. But no Matilda.

In the parking field, a rancher slouched against his touring car, waiting for his daughter. Bert wouldn't have seen him had not he lit his pipe just as Bert happened by.

"Pardon me, sir," Bert jerked to a stop, "but I don't suppose you chanced to see a young lady out here just before the dance broke up?"

"In fact, I did," the rancher replied.

"Did she have on a dark dress--"

"With a white trimming of collar and cuffs," finished the man.

"Where did she go?"

"Well, sir, she was running along fast-like holding hard onto a man's arm. They got in a roadster parked on the hem of the lot and lit out like the boogey man himself was chasing them."

"That wouldn't have been my wife."

"Like as not, it wasn't. I heard the man call her Matilda. They were nigh flying when they passed, and they didn't see me."

Bert's mouth went dry. "My wife's name is Matilda. It could have been that her brother, Michael, came for her. He lives in town. Something must have happened."

"I'd say so," agreed the man, his words marbling around the pipestem.

Bert found Mr. Davis and asked to be taken directly home. "My wife rode on in with someone else," he said. "She may have become ill."

"A mother who is not accustomed to leaving her youngster gets ill every time," chuckled Mr. Davis. "But I would have been glad to take her had she asked."

Bert sat forward in the carriage, trying to will it to go faster. If Matilda was sick, he needed to be with her. At the boardinghouse, he gave Mr. Davis a sawed-off thanks, grabbed his violin case, and ran for the apartment. When only blackness and silence greeted him, he pounded on Mrs. Neuse's door.

The sleep-drugged woman answered his knock with an acrimonious frown. "You don't have to beat my door down, Mr. Conner. You will awaken everyone in the neighborhood! You can just leave your baby until morning at no extra charge. He's tucked in and comfortable. There's no need to disturb him. Mrs. Conner can pick him up before breakfast." She closed the door before he had time to say more.

Bert stumbled back to his quarters, trying to calm himself. Some emergency had arisen. Someone in Matilda's family needed her. That was it. Perhaps her grandmother had died. The whole family had a great love and respect for the elderly Mrs. Harris. Matilda mentioned her often.

Matilda would be in soon and explain everything. She trusted him enough to know that he would care for Little Henry until she returned. He should pull himself together and rest so he could stand by her in the family crisis. His solicitations at such a time might atone for his past neglect.

Without removing his clothing, Bert lay across the bed. Fatigue claimed his body and mind, and he slept in dreamless nothingness until the sun's rays slanted in the east window. His mind was still disentangling itself from the web of sleep when Mrs. Neuse called through the door. "Mrs. Conner?"

Bert's rising was more like a leap. What did the landlady want? Where was Matilda? He hurried to the door, clothes rumpled and hair askew.

Mrs. Neuse held Little Henry in her arms. "I brought----" She narrowed her eyes and glared at Bert. "Have you been drinking, Mr. Conner? That is one thing I absolutely will not tolerate in my tenants. It is grounds for immediate eviction. I will----"

"I have not had a drop to drink, Mrs. Neuse."

"Then what is the problem?"

"I----" Bert faltered, remembering the evening before in one nightmarish flash. Should he tell Mrs. Neuse that he didn't know where his wife might be? He didn't want to lay Matilda's good name on a gossip eager tongue.

"Is Mrs. Conner here? I'd like to speak with her, please."

"She--she isn't here."

"Where is she?"

"I don't know. There may have been a family tragedy."

"You are inebriated, Mr. Conner!"

"No, I----"

"Then you had better come clean with me."

"Matilda left the--the place where we were last night and didn't return. I thought she missed Little Henry and came home ahead of me. But when I arrived, she wasn't here. I suppose her brother came for her or--or something. I thought she would be back before now. I'm--I'm quite worried. Normally, she would have sent word."

"I think I would be worried, too, Mr. Conner."

Her knowing look made Bert ask, "I don't suppose you've heard from her, have you?"

"No, I haven't heard from her directly, but I know young people, and I can add two and two."

"I'm afraid I must ask for enlightenment."

"The young man, your friend, came by trying to find you and Mrs. Conner last evening."

"Pascal?"

"I don't know his name, but he is the one who has visited you much too often since you've roomed here."

"That's Pascal."

"He had fetched himself a roadster and said it was necessary that he locate you. I told him I was caring for the baby while you and the mistress went out to Chalk Mountain for a visit."

The color left Bert's face; he clenched his fists. Why would Matilda leave with Pascal? Was it preplanned? A demon of suspicion leeched onto his soul.

"I--she. . ."

"You don't have to make excuses for her. *I've* lived long enough to know what happened. You brought your friend in time after time. He and your wife fell in love. *You* neglected her and *he* attentioned her. You were too busy with your education and self interests to take notice of what was happening.

"It's the age-old story, Mr. Conner. When a woman gets shut in by four walls with diapers and a dishrag, she'll get restless and break the halter every time. What did you ever give her or do for her? Did you buy her a new hat in all these months of matrimony? Did you bring her a bouquet of roses?

"Who did Mr. Conner think about? Mr. Conner, that's who! A'many a'time I thought, 'The poor girl, she never even gets to go to *church*. She must be rusting out inside. How much longer can she bear it?'

"So I'm not a whit surprised that she ran off with your friend and left you with diapers and a dishrag for a while. I can hardly find it in my generous soul to blame her."

"She knew that I--I would be graduated in three months, and then----"

"Three months can be an infinity to a woman as heart-starved as that one was. Don't think I couldn't hear her crying day after day," exaggerated the troublemaker. "You pushed her over the brink, Mr. Conner, and I find it difficult to have any sympathy for the likes of you."

"Please be excused, Mrs. Neuse. I will care for my son myself. And if I need you again, I will call." Bert lifted his child from her arms.

The woman backed away, a maddening smugness written across her features. To end her visual censure, Bert closed the door abruptly.

He could be glad it was Saturday with no classes to miss. Matilda would be back by Monday, and. . . He chopped the thought in half.

Numbly, he placed Henry in his highchair, wondering what babies ate for breakfast. The remains of Matilda's cake made for 'their night alone' sat on the cupboard's side shelf. That would have to do for now. He opened the pantry to see what he could find and was appalled to find it almost bare. Matilda hadn't mentioned that they were running so dangerously short of food. The budget had been tight for weeks now, but. . .

Matilda. He turned about and saw the picture of her that he had painted when they were first wed. *My First Love.* It mocked him.

A cry of rage brust from his throat. Matilda had double-crossed him! She had run off with Pascal! The pain would have been less had it been anyone but Pascal. His wife had disgraced him. *How could you do this to me, Matilda? So that's why you were so eager to go with me. You were really going for Pascal. You dressed up for him! And I made it easy for both of you. The secret. . . you were going to tell me that you'd had enough, that you'd found love elsewhere.*

Bert rammed his fist into the picture, sending it to the floor with a shattering of glass. Frightened, Little Henry started to cry. And Bert cried with him.

Chapter Six

The Hospital

Vinnie Campbell sat beside Matilda the entire night, and when the girl was none improved by morning, she became alarmed.

"Farley," she said to her husband, "this girl has injuries past the seeing. She still has no response. We need to get her to a doctor. Her folks are doubtless on a search for her now, not knowing where she fell from the wagon. The sooner we can get her alert, the sooner we can know who she is and where she belongs."

"We'll take her, my good woman," Farley Campbell said. "Gather all the pillows you can find so the ride will be soft for her." He hefted Matilda into his hard, muscled arms as if she were made of fine china. "I'm glad for that west wind to temper the chill."

It was five miles in to town. The hospital, a small stone building, squatted on a hill facing west a few blocks from the railroad. The doctor had gone home for a weekend rest, but the hospital was open, supervised by a white-capped nurse. The mortician was removing a body.

The nurse apologized to Mrs. Campbell for the doctor's absence. He had spent long hours trying to make comfortable a patient, an older woman with consumption. They had just lost her. She thanked Vinnie for her good Samaritanship and said she would send for the physician. The girl would likely be fine. "Bumps to the head are strange things," she said. "We don't know as much about them as we'd like to know. Major ones can bring minor complications or vice versa."

"We haven't the money to pay for her care," Vinnie said. "We're farmers."

"Oh, don't worry about that! Our good doctor has never turned away anyone who needed treatment. He says if he doesn't get his pay from earthlings, God will make up the difference. And He always does. Why, just last year a benevolent patient donated a large sum to our institution to make it an even better place for the suffering. You know, Mrs. Campbell, in years gone by, hospitals were terrible places. They were called pesthouses. Do you remember that?"

"Indeed, I do."

"They were for the indigent and friendless, and few people got out alive. But all that has changed, thanks be! Now we have anesthesia, surgery and *cleanliness*. Why, I had to have a nursing school certificate just to work here." She tapped a finger on her badge. "This hospital has a reputation of being the best for miles around."

"Yes, I told Farley that the girl would receive excellent care at Dr. White's clinic," Vinnie avowed.

"Absolutely."

"We will check back the next time we are in town though she will likely be out and gone by then."

Farley Campbell reasoned that they ought to put out word about the girl. "Somebody'll be worried crazy," he said. He suggested that if she fell from a wagon of churchgoers, the parson might know her family. The Mr. John Brown had mentioned the brush arbor meeting. That would be the one going on at Moody. There were no other revivals in progress in the vicinity. It would take some time, but they could call on the preacher.

The minister tried to be helpful but was baffled. He said he recalled every visitor to the service the night before. The crowd was pitifully short, and he could name everyone who attended. There was certainly no young lady clad in a dark green dress with white accessories.

"Mr. Brown said that he was there," spoke up Vinnie.

"Mr. Brown?"

"That is the young man who found the girl beside the road."

"Can you describe him?"

"I didn't get a good look at his face, but he was of medium build and nicely dressed. He was driving a motor car."

"A car? There were no cars here last evening. Only a few horses and buggies."

"Is there another arbor meeting in the area?"

He shook his head. "None in this part of Texas as far as I know."

"Now that stumps me," Vinnie said to Farley as they headed homeward. "Mr. Brown said as clear as day that he found the girl on his way home from the revival meeting."

"Something doesn't ring right, Vinnie," he said. "It's almost as if the young man was trying to rid himself of the girl. I heard the sound of his feet as he left, and he was *running*."

"He was in a rush to get home to his invalid mother. He said so."

"I wonder. . . ."

They stopped at several dwellings along the road, but no one had inquired at any of the farmhouses for a lost girl. "Do you suppose she's an angel, Farley?" suggested Vinnie.

"I'd come nearer thinking John Brown was a devil," her husband rejoined.

Meanwhile, Pascal had parked his vehicle at a roadside turnout which was little more than a patch of gravel and slept away a hangover. His head still throbbed when he awoke, but his senses were clear. The bent fender served to remind him of the previous night's wreck, and he was more terrified sober than he had been while intoxicated. Bert would make hash of him if Matilda was seriously injured! He had done a foolish thing when he lured Matilda away from the dance. Ah, the wages of foolishness! He'd best get Matilda back to her spouse and on the double!

What did the lady say? Pascal furrowed his brow in a desperate effort to remember Vinnie Campbell's words. Oh, yes! She said she would take Matilda to Dr. White's hospital in Garden City. He could go there, get her dismissed, and take her back to Walnut Springs today. He'd make up a convincing lie for the doctor. He'd say he was Matilda's brother and his folks sent him for her.

Then when she woke up, he would take her and put her out near Mrs. Neuse's boardinghouse and leave the country. Bert would never find him.

Who needed a friend like Bert Conner anyway? A friend who would run in ahead of you and steal your girl and refuse to give you a key to his apartment? Some friend!

Pascal parked his car, forgetting to turn the damaged side away from the front view of the hospital. He walked in as if he owned the place. That was Pascal's way. Barge in. Bluff. Act professional. It worked wonders.

The nurse glanced up from the chart she was studying. "Can I help you, sir?"

"I'm looking for Matilda Conner."

"Matilda Conner?" Having lost a patient but a few hours ago, the nurse had a somber countenance. "She isn't here."

Pascal's train of thought ran amok. Mrs. Campbell had said she would bring Matilda to the clinic. He had no doubts that she had. But something had gone wrong. Matilda must have been injured internally, and she had *died*.

"Did--did anyone die this morning?" Pascal pressed.

The nurse hesitated. The pause spoke volumes. "Are you a family member?" she asked.

"I am. I am her brother."

"I am sorry," the nurse said, real pity in her voice. "I didn't realize she had a brother so, ah, young." She patted his arm. "You do understand that we did everything we could, don't you? In these terminal cases, we feel very helpless. We. . . we tried to make her comfortable to the end. You can be solaced in the assurance that she was a true Christian and is at rest in a better place. Her suffering is over."

"Did--did she regain consciousness?"

"No. She was too low when we got her."

"Where will she be buried?"

"They took her body to Brewster's Funeral Parlor. I'm sure you will want to go there to help with the arrangements. Do you know where that is?"

"Yes." Tears pooled in Pascal's eyes.

He left the hospital with the conviction that he didn't want to view Matilda's corpse. He had killed her, and she was too young to die. The thought of her death brought his own mortality into unblemished focus. It was something he couldn't face, didn't wish to dwell on.

Matilda was dead. It was so absolute it closed over him like an airless tomb. He'd never see her again. The incident chased Pascal, haunting him. He roamed about, staying in sheds and vacant buildings, seldom allowing himself a moment without the bracing effect of his grog. Matilda's face filled his dreams by night, became a phantom by day.

The nurse had been deeply affected by Pascal's sorrow. She mentioned the young man to the doctor when he came to check on Matilda. "Mrs. Terezick's brother came by shortly after the hearse picked up her body, Doctor. He seemed exceptionally disturbed by the death."

"Her brother?"

"Yes. I sent him to the funeral parlor."

"Mrs. Terezick's *brother*? Mrs. Terezick didn't have a brother. She had three older sisters."

"This was a very young man. Twentyish. He was driving a nice roadster with the exception of a badly crunched fender."

"Mrs. Terezick was fifty-four. Could he have been a nephew, perhaps?"

"He said he was her brother, and he left weeping."

The doctor scratched his head. "There is a mistake somewhere. We'll let the undertaker straighten that one out. But you called for me to see a new patient?"

"Yes, sir. The girl was brought in comatose."

"Have we any medical history?" The doctor, a gracious and confident man, was one of those rare practitioners whose physical appearance matched his intelligence and ability.

"None, sir. We don't know her name, her age, or her address. Mrs. Campbell, the lady who brought her for admission, said a man left the girl at her house in the middle of the night. The man's story was that she had fallen from a wagon on the way home from church and he happened to see her stumbling along in the ditch, somewhat disoriented.

"I haven't been able to rouse her since she arrived. She has a lump on her head as if she had struck it on something."

"I'm surprised that her family hasn't been here to inquire already."

"The whole case is quite unorthodox and poses a mystery, I'm afraid."

"I'll have a look at her."

The nurse stood beside the doctor as he bent over Matilda and gently moved her limbs. He lifted one eyelid to have a look at her pupil then felt cautiously for broken ribs. With his stethoscope, he listened to her heart and her lungs.

He straightened up. "She's had a blow to the head. How serious it is, I don't know. Her body is slightly swollen. Everything else checks out fine. Let's not jostle her around for awhile. Get her into something comfortable and let her rest. Likely as not, she will rally on her own in a few hours. We'll keep a close watch on her."

"She's a pretty thing, isn't she? She has gorgeous hair!"

"She is in good physical condition. Her color is good. Her vital signs are excellent. How old would you take her to be?"

"Scarcely out of her teens."

"That was my guess."

"It seems funny not to have a name to write on her chart."

"Yes, she's the first Jane Doe we've ever had, but I don't expect she'll stay nameles. Someone will claim her soon."

The nurse smiled. "If someone doesn't, I will, Doctor."

CHAPTER SEVEN

Bert's Decision

Catching a ride the short distance to Brazos Point would pose no problem. Some of the country community's populace came in for supplies every Saturday, and about once a month, the Gibsons brought their wagon to town. Bert couldn't remember how long it had been since their last trip.

After he'd absorbed the initial shock of Matilda's leaving, Bert pulled himself together. He had to make some decisions for his future and his son's. He had few options. He could discontinue his education and be relegated to a common laborer's wages, or he could press on to graduation and get a degree that would command higher pay. For himself, he could manage with little. But he had a son to feed, clothe, and send to school. Without the help of a wife, it wouldn't be easy.

The quandary chafed his mind all morning, but by noon he had made up his mind. He *must* complete his college courses. His widowed mother had sacrificed much on his behalf, and he couldn't disappoint her. It would be a cruel injustice to waste her hard-earned investment. She had worked a full-time job to see him through the academy.

It hadn't been fair of him to marry Matilda and conceal the marriage from his mother. Now, when his mother came to his graduation exercises and found that he was a father--and that his wife had walked away with Pascal--she would be set back on her heels. She might be hurt and angry and with good reason. He supposed Matilda's desertion served him right for his dishonesty.

Surely the raw places would scab over with time. Little Henry had begged for his mother all morning. How long would it take for the purgative of infantile forgetfulness to wash away the child's tears?

The best thing to do, Bert decided, was to ask the baby's maternal grandmother, Sarah Gibson, to keep him for the three months until school's termination. He had no doubts that she would do it and gladly. Little Henry would be close by so that he could go to see his son any time he grew homesick for the child.

His efforts at getting Henry's stockings on were clumsy and slow. Henry wouldn't sit still. The child kept repeating "Mama. . . Mama" like a broken phonograph cylinder.

"We're going to Grandma's," Bert explained, but Henry had spent little time with anyone except Matilda, and the words had no meaning. "Mama!" he howled with increased volume.

Bert rolled the boy's clothing into a bundle, picked him up, and put the four blocks to the town's center behind him with a determined stride. Telling Mrs. Gibson that her daughter had been unfaithful would be no pleasant task, but life didn't promise a painless path. A man did what he must however unpleasant.

He winced as Jacob's Drugstore shouldered up, taller than the buildings around it. It resurrected memories of the girl with the crown of brown-gold hair. The girl with the clear, trusting eyes. Behind the soda counter was where he had met Matilda. . . .

The Springs had become a commerce center, fresh and elemental by reason of the new railroad. Tracks ran through the middle of town. Across the tracks in the little park with its natural springs, he and Matilda had picnicked, had walked hand in hand. . . .

Today, the town was crowded with people from Morgan, Eulogy, Bono, Flat Top. Horses, buggies and wagons lined Main Street until there were no empty hitching posts. Some Model T's and a few Model A's were parked here and there. Newcomers tipped their hats to each other, not sure who had affluence and who didn't.

History was moving to the end of an era. Noise and exhaust fumes filled the air. Modernism levied the tribute, and society paid the toll.

A little burnt crust of a man with bulldog jaws hurried toward Bert. He was dressed in black, his slim cravat slightly off-center. A massive hat blotted out the scenery behind him, and a diamond stickpin in his lapel served its intended purpose of calling attention to itself. "Aren't you Mr. Conner?" the man asked.

"Yes, I am," Bert replied.

"I believe you are a friend of a young rebel named Pascal."

"The person of whom you speak is no longer my friend." The words arrived much icier than Bert sent them.

"Oh, he double-crossed you, too, did he?"

"That's a mild phrase for what he did to me."

"Do you know where I might find him?"

"I have no idea, nor do I have any wish to know." Bert pulled Little Henry closer to him.

"Well, look here, Mr. Conner. This Pascal fellow made a deal to buy my roadster. It was an expensive automobile. He asked to test drive it down the road a ways before he gave me the money. He didn't return from the trial run, and I haven't seen him or the car since."

Bert gave a brittle laugh, a laugh that carried no mirth. "Be glad that's all you lost, Mister." He turned aside to go around the man.

"If you see him, Mr. Conner, please tell him that Mr. Spratt is turning him in to the county sheriff for theft."

"I won't see him."

Bert thought he could spot Hank Gibson's wagon among the ocean of wagons if, indeed, Hank and Sarah had come to town today. He walked down one side of the street and had started up the other when he came face to face with Mr. Gibson as Hank emerged from the post office.

"Bert!" his father-in-law waved a greeting. "I had planned to come by. Sarah didn't come to town with me today, but she sent a package for Matilda----"

Bert's frown stopped Mr. Gibson mid-sentence. "I can give the parcel to you to take to her if you'd rather I don't come by."

Bert said nothing, so Hank continued.

"We're having a birthday party for Grandmother Harris, and Sarah wanted me to give Matilda the word." The glower still camped on Bert's face, immovable. "Is--is Matilda well?" Hank Gibson faltered.

"I don't know. If it isn't asking too much, Mr. Gibson, I'd like to ride out to your place with you and talk with Matilda's mother."

"Certainly, Bert. I'll hurry with the list Sarah sent, and we'll go directly. You'll bring the baby along?"

"Yes."

"Sarah will be glad to see him."

"May I go on to the wagon? Little Henry is getting sleepy."

"Make yourself comfortable."

Bert was mute on the way to Brazos Point. Hank, a man of few words himself, respected the silence into which Bert had retreated. They knew little about each other, these two. Their worlds orbited in different galaxies. The old wagon, bouncing its way home, made its own conversation as it complained across the valley clad in soft brown wool.

The day was chilly, but the air gave a hint of spring. Matilda had talked about springtime in the country, her favorite time of the year. It was Matilda who saw the beauty in the river that nibbled its way through the field, the arthritic trees with their swollen joints, the bluebonnets with their spendthrift blooms. It was Matilda who. . .

A covey of quail whirred up in front of the wagon, a rabbit sprinted away and a hawk scolded. There was abundant life all about him, but Bert felt nothing. His heart was dry and hard. The seasons obeyed some eternal cycle, but he was locked into the dead of winter.

Sarah met them at the door. Bert was glad that Sarah's daughter bore little resemblance to her. Hers was not a face from which her daughter's had been copied. Sarah was a striking woman in her own rights, but Matilda did not favor her. The mother had black hair that clung to her head, straight and thick, while her daughter's tresses, the color of a new penny, were wavy and eager to be spent in the breeze. Sarah's eyes were dark while Matilda's were a sparkling green.

"Bert!" Sarah reached out her arms for Little Henry. "What a lovely surprise! I had been yearning to see my grandson. Matilda got the message, I guess----" She glanced about, bewildered. "Where is Matilda?"

"Please, let's go inside and sit down, Mrs. Gibson."

"Oh, don't tell me that something dreadful has happened to my Matilda!" pled Sarah, her face draining of all color.

"No, something dreadful has happened to *me*," Bert said.

Sarah's hands would not be still. She patted the baby and soothed his back. Then she ran her fingers through his hair. "Tell us, Bert, and we'll do our best to help. After all, you are our Matilda's husband, our own son-in-law. Is it a matter of health or finances or----"

"Mrs. Gibson, your daughter left me. She ran off with a man that I have befriended since grammar school. It is a blow with which I have had a hard time coming to grips."

Sarah gave a cry of protest. "No, it can't be true! There is a mistake somewhere. Matilda would never do a thing like that. I taught her better."

"She is gone, Mrs. Gibson. I have all the evidence I need. She was seen leaving with him." Bert turned to Hank. "You believe me, don't you, Mr. Gibson?" It was a sincere appeal.

"I. . . it isn't easy to believe that one's own daughter would commit such a--such a sin."

Why Bert should feel that he must defend Matilda, or at the least bear some of the blame, he could not have explained even to himself. His tongue seemed to be disconnected from his brain. "Don't lay all the blame on her, Mrs. Gibson. I'm afraid that I was too absorbed with my own problems, my classes and work and travel to give her enough of myself. And, too, I went overboard in trying to help this--this friend who ran off with my wife."

"But even if Matilda would leave you, she would never leave her baby!" objected Sarah. "Matilda loved her baby more than she loved her own life."

"I know that it doesn't make sense, and I know it is a shock to you. I'm still wrestling with the facts myself. Unfaithfulness is a hard concept to acknowledge."

"She just left Little Henry alone and walked away?"

"We had gone to a party. Pascal showed up at the party, and she left with him from there. She did not return home."

"Pascal," repeated Sarah. "She told me once that she didn't

care for this Pascal."

"She kept her sentiment for him well hidden. Pascal bought --or stole--a roadster. Maybe that turned her head. We hadn't been able to afford even a surrey. With the expense of books, we had few extras."

"*Things* shouldn't matter," argued Hank. "Marriage is for better or for worse--and forever besides. Matilda wasn't brought up with a great deal of finery. We live a simple life."

"I had promised her that things would be better after I finished my schooling. We discussed our future before we left for the party, and she seemed willing to see me through these last few weeks. In fact, she made me promise not to curtail my education for any reason. I can't believe I lost her just three months before I could start treating her as she deserved."

"Mama will die when she hears this," moaned Sarah, "and right here before her birthday celebration!"

"Do you plan to continue your classes?" asked Hank. "You are so near now----"

"Yes, I will finish. I cannot disappoint my mother. She has spent a great sum to see that I have a proper education."

"Who will keep Little Henry?"

Bert cleared his throat. "That's why I came today. I wondered if I might leave him here with you for these final weeks."

Sarah buried her face in Henry's hair, smothering his auburn curls with kisses. "Oh, yes, yes, Bert! I will take the very best care of him! It will be a bittersweet joy."

Hank, a big man bronzed to the color of the landscape, walked over and laid his work-grizzled hand on Bert's shoulder. "We've never become acquainted, Bert. I know nothing of your past. But it is the future that counts, and you can count on me as if I were your own father."

Bert lowered his head to hide the silent tears. The hand on his shoulder, the low-pitched voice, the love and warmth, . . . It took Bert back to the day of his father's death, the day he decided he would make it on his own--without God.

Chapter Eight

A New Name

"What do you think, Doctor?" The nurse joined him beside Matilda's bed. "She swallows the water and the broth I give her. She responds to simple commands. She is moving around more."

"Retha, it is in God's hands. There is only so much a doctor can do. She may wake up tomorrow, and then again, she may never wake up. I'm afraid I have less hope every day. It has been a week now, hasn't it?"

"Yes, it was a week yesterday. If she rallies, will she remember what happened?"

"She may and she may not. Every closed head injury is a riddle all its own. There are no formulas, patterns or pat answers. The medical journals are little help. We will keep her comfortable --and pray." He made notes on Matilda's chart. "Has there been *no one* call on her?"

"No one, sir."

The doctor shook his head as if to clear a fog from his mind. "This is the most baffling case in my entire practice. Here is a beautiful girl, well-dressed and apparently loved, and no search is being made for her."

Before she left the room, Retha Bennis brushed Matilda's

hair, tying it back with a blue ribbon she had brought from home. The hairbow made the girl look even younger, more vulnerable. She felt herself becoming attached to this unknown girl. The doctor was giving up, but she would never give up. Sometime, somehow in God's own time, the pieces of the puzzle would fit together. One didn't live to himself or die to himself. This girl had a family somewhere.

She took Matilda's hand in her own and prayed. "Dear God," she said, "this little lamb belongs to you. We don't know who she is, but You do. Only You can awaken her, and I am asking that You do that. Until then, let me care for her to the best of my ability. Amen." A smile flickered across her patient's face.

When the nurse returned for her routine check an hour later, Matilda's eyes were open. She looked about as if she was lost.

"Oh, my dear! Those eyes are open at last! It is an answer to my prayer! Can I get you anything?" the nurse asked.

"I'm fine, thank you," Matilda answered.

"Let me call the doctor. He will be elated!"

"The doctor?"

"You are in Dr. White's hospital. I am your nurse, Retha. You have had a head injury. Do you remember anything about it?"

"No, ma'am." The words failed to convey any meaning to Matilda.

"We have been waiting a week for you to wake up so you can tell us who you are and where you live. We will contact your family, and they will come for you."

Matilda looked puzzled. "My family?"

"What is your name, dear?"

Tears threatened Matilda's eyes. "I--I can't remember. I'm sorry."

Retha patted her shoulder. "Don't worry about it just yet.

Sometimes memory seeps back slowly. Everything will come to you in due time. Would you like to sit up awhile? You've been lying there for a week. Here, let me help you."

Matilda sat up, still bewildered. "How did I get here?"

"A farmer's wife by the name of Vinnie Campbell brought you. Someone found you beside the road; you had fallen from a wagon."

"Oh. Where did they find me?"

"About five miles east of here."

"Where is 'here'?"

"This is Garden City."

She needs familiar things with which to identify, reasoned the nurse. She went to the closet for Matilda's dress. "You were wearing this dark green dress when you came in. Had you been to church, or were you traveling in the wagon to visit someone?"

Matilda's eyes showed no recognition of the garment. "I--I don't know."

"All you need to do right now is eat well and rest. We will take care of you until your 'rememberer' starts working again," the nurse smiled. "We've been expecting a search party to show up any day with a warrant for a pretty girl."

A mirror! The girl would remember who she was if she could see her own reflection. Retha went for a small mirror and handed it to Matilda. "I've tried to keep that gorgeous hair untangled. Here! See for yourself."

Matilda studied herself in the mirror with a girlish curiosity. Her reflection told her nothing. She ran one hand over her long mane. "It's almost red, isn't it? And my eyes are green! Thank you for brushing my hair."

"How old are you?" Retha asked quickly, hoping some spontaneous reflex would answer for the girl.

"I have no idea. I look grown-up, though, don't I?"

The doctor came and put Matilda through a battery of questions that brought no enlightenment either to himself or to his patient. Did she have a sister? Where did she go to school? What kind of flowers grew in her yard? What kind of work did her father do? Where did she shop for hats? Did she like to ride horses? The girl's mind seemed as empty as a cave deserted by bats.

"What is the prognosis, Doctor?" asked Retha when they were out of Matilda's hearing. "Good or bad?"

"I wish I could answer that," he sighed. "She is suffering from amnesia, a memory loss. There is no way of knowing whether it is permanent or temporary. Amnesia often involves the unconscious suppression of a painful experience and everything connected to it, including their identity. Memory proceeds in two steps, short term and long term. Memory that is lost in trauma or emotional stress can sometimes be reestablished by associations with the past. With this young lady, it hasn't worked. I mentioned a wagon, a fall from a wagon, a dark road at night, hoping to arouse some emotion: fear, anxiety, anger. Nothing. Quite frankly, she has me worried. Maybe I'm expecting too much too soon. I had hoped that hers would be a short trip. . . ."

Retha tried various means of mental therapy on her own. When she brought a Bible, Matilda's eyes lighted with pleasure. "Read your favorite verse to me," the nurse said, excited with her patient's response to the Book.

Matilda immediately turned to Isaiah 40:31 and read: *But they that wait upon the Lord shall renew their strength; they shall mount up with wings as eagles; they shall run, and not be weary; and they shall walk, and not faint.*

"Has that scripture been your favorite since you were a child?" goaded Retha.

"I don't remember anything about my childhood," Matilda answered. "That verse just came to me. There are a lot of other verses I like, too. I love all the Old Testament stories, the prophets, and the Gospels. The Book of Acts gives the plan of salvation. Paul's letters tell us how to live godly in this present world, and Revelation lets us know about the end of time. It's a wonderful Book! I can recite the whole of Psalm 34."

The flawless memory of the Bible amazed Retha. The girl had had thorough religious training. Might her father have been a parson? Some preachers, called "circuit riders," traveled about the country, conducting revivals. The story that she was going home from church when the accident occurred seemed a logical assumption.

When a sick baby was admitted to the clinic for medical attention, Matilda showed an inordinate concern, pumping Retha for information about the baby's welfare. "I love babies," she said. "I can hold him if you need me to. I don't like for a baby to be ill."

Retha reported each development to the doctor. "Let her hold the child, and see what happens," he suggested.

Matilda took the little boy into her arms and began to croon softly to him. He immediately stopped whimpering and fell into a peaceful sleep.

"She has cared for a baby before," the doctor calculated. "Either a sibling or her own. I'll write that on her chart. Piece by piece, we'll put her back together."

Physically, Matilda gained strength at a rapid pace. She resented the confinement to her bed and her room. Retha often found her standing at the front door, peering out into the street. She seemed restless.

"She is ready to be released," the doctor said, "but we have nowhere to send her. I can't bear to see her go to the poorhouse."

"Oh, no, Doctor! We could never send her there," objected the nurse. "I will take her to my home. I still have faith for a complete recovery. Will she be safe--alone? She wouldn't wander off, would she?"

"No, she is quite sane. The past is gone, but the present is intact. When the brain is deprived of one area, it makes another supply the deficiency. She is yours. We can do nothing more for her by keeping her here."

Retha went to Matilda's room. "I'm taking you home with me," she told her. "I live alone, and you will be great company for me. Will you be afraid to stay by yourself in the daytime?"

"I'm not afraid, but I wouldn't be happy just *sitting*," Matilda replied. "I must find a job and pay the bill I have incurred here at the hospital. That would only be right."

"What sort of work did you do before you came here?" It was another subtle attempt to make Matilda's mind bring up the past.

"I don't know. But I suppose I could learn to do most anything. I can read and I can write. I could help you with the hospital work, or I could cook and clean house for some rich lady. Or babysit. I don't want to be a burden, and I want to pay my debt."

"Before he can dismiss you, the doctor says we must come up with a name for you. For his records."

"A name?"

"What shall we name you?"

"Let me think." Matilda found the humor in the situation and gave a lilting laugh. "Not many people get to name themselves after they are grown, do they? How about Linda?"

"I like that. That's a good vanilla name. But what about a surname? You can share mine or choose your own. My name is

Bennis, and there are not many Bennises around. We could use one more."

"That's too complicated. Since my hair is red and my eyes are green, how about Brown for a name? Linda Brown."

"Well, Linda Brown, the doctor thinks you should live with someone for awhile, at least until you are able to support yourself. When my shift is over today, I will show you to your new home. Later on, we will advertise for you a job if you wish."

"That's kind of you," Matilda said. "I hope that it won't take me long to stand on my own two feet."

That afternoon, an errand to town provided an excuse for Vinnie Campbell to call at the hospital. "My curiosity has me by the nape of the neck, Farley," she said to her husband. "I'd like to learn the fate of our Sleeping Beauty."

"We'll go by," he said.

The nurse greeted Mrs. Campbell cordially, hoping that the woman might have some additional information on the unidentified patient. "She has regained consciousness and is doing quite well," Retha told her, "but she has amnesia. She doesn't remember any of her past life. The doctor is releasing her today, and I am taking her to stay with me for a few days. It is our hopes that her memory will return."

"If she needs a change of scenery, she may visit me," Vinnie offered. "I find it most disturbing that no one has come looking for her."

"Yes, it is very irregular. It is obvious that she is wellbred; she has good manners. I find her courteous and--and courtly, that's the word. Someone lost a jewel."

"I will say hello to her if I may."

"By all means. She enjoys people. She has made a friend of all the patients who have come and gone. She especially likes children," Retha informed. "She's in Room Three."

Vinnie started to walk away.

"Oh, and by the way, she named herself Linda. Linda Brown."

Vinnie whirled about. "Brown?"

"She said Brown would be a good, colorful name since her hair is red and her eyes are green."

"Brown was the name of the young man who brought her to me. John Brown."

"And then he. . . left?"

"He left running."

"Oh----" Retha groaned. "I'm afraid this further complicates the matter."

"Do you suppose John Brown was her brother? Or her husband? Could she be a victim of abuse? Or abandonment?" Vinnie wore her thoughts on the outside. "He declared he didn't know her. However, his other talk didn't pan out to be true. He said he'd been to the brush arbor meeting, and when we checked out his story, it wasn't so."

"And you don't know where he was from, Mrs. Campbell?" urged Retha.

"Wait!" Vinnie furrowed her brow. "Now I remember that Mr. Brown said he had to rush on to Belton because his widowed mother was at home alone and would be worried about him."

"That's a clue!" cheered Retha.

Matilda walked the short distance to the nurse's station to speak to Retha about her only dress. It was becoming too small for her. Seeing that the nurse had a customer, she turned to go back to her room.

"Linda!" called Retha. "This is Mrs. Campbell, the lady who brought you here when you were injured. She has met someone who may be related to you. Does 'John Brown' ring a bell?"

Matilda looked blank. "John Brown? No, ma'am. I've never heard of him. I don't suppose Brown is my real name; it's just a name I made up. I--I wish I could remember *something*."

"One day soon, I will come and take you back to the place of the accident," Vinnie said. "Retracing your steps might help."

"I hope so."

The girl's naming herself Brown might not be a coincidence, thought the nurse. In hopes of a breakthrough, she sent letters of inquiry to every Brown listed on the Bell County register. The dark threads of uncertainty that held her patient's mind a prisoner must be severed.

Chapter Nine

Number Forty-Three

Matilda's disappearance consumed Martha Harris' thoughts. She cried and prayed and cried some more. "Sally!" she'd say. "Stop what you're doin' an' let's me an' you *pray* fer little Tilly."

"I do pray, Mama," Sally would reply. "I pray morning and night, but if I stop for a prayer meeting every time you think about Matilda, I'll not get my work--or yours--done."

"Souls are more important than warshin' clothes or cookin' mush or churnin' butter."

"Yes, Mama, but fixing meals is necessary if I'm to keep your body alive so you can keep on worrying about all of us." Sally's barbs were always wrapped with loving consideration, and Martha understood that.

"Sally, do you honest b'lieve that Tilly jest up an' run off from her own husband an' baby 'cause she didn't love nor want them no more?"

"I'm not the judge of Matilda's motives, Mama. Matilda's nature doesn't match such actions, but the facts are there, and it's hard to dispute cold, hard statistics. Sarah has Little Henry as proof that Matilda deserted him."

"You don't s'pose she was kidnapped?"

"Mama! What will you think of next?"

"It's not unheard of! Don't you remember when our own little crippled Effie was kidnapped?"

"That was different. Those wild Grimes boys wanted some quick cash, so they tied Effie up in the old barn. I wouldn't exactly call that a----"

"It was a kidnap, alright. They left th' ransom note on th' dressin' table in Effie's room."

"If you're thinking Claude Grimes took Matilda, he didn't. Claude has been in prison for years, and he has years yet to go."

"He mayhap escaped or got out early on good behavin' an' still wants some money from us. So he coulda up an' decided on gettin' Tilly this time an' scarin' Bert's friend into doin' th' job for him. Mayhap he threatened Bert's friend with a gun. Mayhap----"

"There's not a chance, Mama. Claude robbed a federal bank. They have tight security and don't let those kind of criminals out early."

"Well, anyhow, mayhap you'd better look around on th' dressin' tables for a ransom note jest in case."

"I dusted all the tables this morning."

"You know, sometimes my mind does somersaults backerds, Sally, an' I remember th' past as if'n it was yesterday. So much has happened to us Harrises that I think we could write a long, thick book."

"Nobody would read it."

"I ain't so sure, Sally-girl. Dessie writ a piece fer her schoolwork about Effie's kidnapping an' named it *Love's Golden Wings*. Th' teacher give her a' A+ on it. Dessie always kept th' most innerestin' diaries."

"What were you doing snooping into Dessie's diaries?"

Martha's expression was that of a cat caught in the cream. "It was jest a *few* times."

Keep her mind off Matilda, Sally. "Dessie did love to write."

"We could take her journal an' tell about how Effie saved yore life an' won our hearts."

"She already had everybody's heart but yours. Especially Joseph's and Dessie's."

"We'd call that book *To Love a Bent-Winged Angel* 'cause that's what Joseph always called Effie."

"I remember."

"But I wouldn't want Dessie tellin' how mean I was to Effie; I can't bear to even think on it now. I thought she was cursed 'cause she was born crippled."

"In a book, you have to tell the good and the bad. That's what makes a good book."

"Then let's skip that'n an' do up one about Effie after she started to school, tellin' how smart she was an' all about her big heart an' how as she built us this house with her inheritance. Then we could write about you runnin' away to th' city like the prodigal son an' name it *To Love a Runaway* 'cause I loved you even if you did run away an'----"

"Leave me out of it, Mama. Nobody wants to hear about a juvenile delinquent!"

Martha, caught up in her reverie, rambled on. "An' wouldn't th' story of Candice huntin' for little Chessica make a grand book? We could name it *Two Scars Against One*. An' we could make a whole volume on--"

Sarah came through the front door, holding Little Henry by the hand. "Knock, knock," she called, and the child mimicked the words.

"Sarey!" Martha almost shouted. "We think we'll write us some books."

Sarah looked to Sally for an explanation. "Is Mama okay?"

Martha's mind jumped back to her original concern. "We think mayhap Matilda was kidnapped for a ransom like Effie was an'----"

"Bert knows when Matilda left and with whom. She was seen leaving with his best friend," Sarah said. "A rancher saw her, described what she was wearing, and heard Bert's friend call her by her name."

"I can't make myself b'lieve a granddaughter o' mine would be so wicked. An' t' think she was onct a Christian an' sang in our own church. I can't make no sense of it, Sarey."

"Mama gone-gone," Little Henry said.

"Poor little motherless lamb," grieved Martha. "What is this world a-comin' to? Better that Tilly had died an' been buried out yonder with yer first baby an' her gran'pa, Sarey, than to come to sech perdition. How can you stand it?"

"Only by God's grace, Mama. Every morning I ask for help to get through another day. I have to hold up for the baby."

"Leastwise, with you raisin' him, he'll get a chance t' be taken to church an' learn about Jesus."

"I'm afraid I won't get to raise him."

"What do you mean?"

"I'm just keeping him until his father finishes his college work. Then he plans to take the baby with him to wherever he relocates."

"You mean, he's takin' Little Henry away? He--who plays fer dances an' don't have a thought of God--is goin' t' raise my great-grandson?"

"Legally, Henry belongs to Bert. Hank says it is likely that we will lose track of the child when Bert takes him."

"It's too grievous! Do you think, Sarey, that Tilly will ever come home to see you? Do you think she'll come to see me 'fore I die?"

"Yes, Mama. I trained her right. When she is older, she will come to herself like the prodigal did."

"But I may not be 'round by then. I'm losin' ground ever' day."

Sarah turned her face away. What her mother said was true. Martha had grown considerably more feeble in the past year. She would soon join her husband in the churchyard. This worry over Matilda might finish her off.

"I hope she'll change her mind. . . soon," Sarah said. Her voice was low and strained.

"Do you think her husband would have her back?"

"I don't know, but I believe he would. He is near out of his wits about her. Actually, he is a nice man, Mama. He and Hank have established a friendship through this misfortune."

"Do you s'pose Bert would come to the Harris reunion? With Easter in April this year, we'll be gettin' t'gether 'fore his school lets out."

"I doubt if he would be comfortable around our family after the way Matilda hurt him. But I'll invite him."

"Does he come to see Little Henry every weekend?"

"Yes. He catches a ride out on Saturday and walks back on Sunday. Hank has offered time and again to tote him back and forth in the wagon, but Bert insists on doing it his way. He's independent."

"You don't think he'll tire of the child?"

"No, he loves his son." She rummaged about in the diaper bag. "He brings a newspaper for Hank when he comes. I thought you might enjoy it, too. Sally can read it to you."

After Sarah left, Martha asked for the newpaper. With her

dimmed eyesight, she could read only the larger headlines. Sally found her squinting at an article.

"Read this to me, Sally," she said, pointing to an item about the state government. "My Alan works for 'em there at Austin."

Sally read the column aloud. Martha understood little of the legislative jargon but nodded her head as if she did. "I'm proud of Alan," she said.

"The news isn't about Alan's department."

Martha could be conveniently deaf when she wished. "There's a piece on th' inside I was innerested in. About th' search."

Sally thumbed through the paper. "*Statewide Search for Relatives of Girl.* Is that it? On page five?"

"That's the one I want to hear."

"'An intensive search is being launched for the relatives of a young woman who suffered an apparent head injury,'" Sally read. "'She has no recall of her past. She was admitted to Dr. White's hospital in Temple in a comatose condition but has since regained consciousness. She has reddish brown hair, green eyes, and appears to be around twenty years of age. It is reported that the woman was discovered on State Road 317 near Moody and that she possibly fell from a wagon in that vicinity. Anyone with information concerning her or her family may contact the hospital or the newspaper office.'"

"You don't s'pose that could be our Tilly?"

"Of course not, Mama! This is a Fort Worth paper. This didn't happen around here. If something bad had happened to Matilda, Bert would be notified."

"Anyway, I'm gonna pray about that," Martha stated. "What if'n it *was* one o' my own daughters or granddaughters that was hurt in th' head an' didn't know nothin'?"

"Mama! If you're going to take on the worries of the whole

State of Texas, I will stop reading the newspaper to you! You don't even know the girl!"

"Mayhap I don't. But God does! An' it won't hurt none to add one more on t' my prayin' list. She'll be number forty-three."

Sally threw up her hands in exasperation. "So be it. Miss Anonymous will please take number forty-three and wait."

CHAPTER TEN

The Urn

Pascal, in various stages of inebriation, visited the cemetery daily. Since the accident, his remiss conscience had been unrelenting.

He found a recent mound of dirt that bore no headstone and decided it was Matilda's grave. On the hillock, he sat and talked to her, making profuse apologies. When he had exhausted his vocabulary of regrets, he busied himself with making endless excuses for his actions and then discounting them all. His séance ended with his talking to Bert, begging his pardon. Hours of each day were thus spent at the city burial grounds.

On one of these occasions, an elderly lady with a cane alighted from a vehicle and hobbled up to Pascal. He had his head cradled on his arms, asleep. She cracked him across the shoulders with her walking stick. "What are you doing here, young man?" she croaked.

Pascal's head jerked up. "I'm--I'm visiting the grave of a friend, ma'am. I come here every day."

"What friend?"

"Matilda Conner."

"This isn't Matilda Conner's grave. This is my sister's grave."

"It's--it's a new grave, and there was no marker----"

"We haven't set the stone yet, but her name was Terezick. Lonita Terezick. She was named for our father, Lonnie Terezick. She was an old maid. No man came nigh her when she was alive, and she wouldn't want one nigh now. So scram."

"But I thought--that is, this is the only fresh grave around. Is there another cemetery somewhere?"

"There's the county's acre where they bury people who are too poor to pay for a lot."

"Where is that?"

The lady ignored him. "Most of the time, though, they just incinerate the bodies of the indigent. That's cheaper."

"Incinerate them?"

"Yes, sir. They burn them to cinders. Then they put their ashes in a clay pot. They call it an urn."

"And what do they do with the. . . pot?"

If the woman heard him, she gave no indication of it. "Move along now, laddie. I want to weep in private for my baby sister. She was so generous! She left her false teeth to me. Mourning is a personal thing."

Pascal backed away. So they turned Matilda to charcoal, did they? Naturally, they would look for the cheapest way to dispose of her. Nobody knew who she was; there was no one to pay for her burial. He would need to find out where her ashes were.

On unstable legs, Pascal made his way to the funeral parlor to speak to the mortician.

"Do you burn bodies of the dead here?" he asked.

"Are you talking about cremation?" the undertaker queried.

"No, not creation. In-sinner-something."

"Incineration. We call it cremation. It is the process of rendering a deceased beloved to beautiful distinction for safekeeping."

"Do you do that here?"

"No, sir, we send the bodies to a crematorium."

"Where?"

"We send them to Dallas."

"And then they send them back here?"

"If the family wishes. We try to accommodate the bereaved to the best of our ability. Some request that the ashes be kept in a mausoleum; others wish to take the remains to their homes. We've even been asked to scatter the ashes in the quiet of the woods or place them on the surface of a peaceful lake.

"It is those who are left behind that we try to placate. Sometimes the loved one makes his or her wishes known before they expire. Cremation is generally less expensive than a casket type of laying away. And there is another advantage: If one moves a great distance, one can take the residue of their dear one along with them. Have you, ah, someone who is interested in the process?"

"No, I just wondered," Pascal paused and looked about wildly. "Uh, I wondered how it worked. Thank you."

He started out of the morgue. As he did, a ceramic flower pot beside the front door caught his eye. *That's Matilda's ashes,* his booze-soaked mind persisted. *They sat them there hoping someone would claim them. And nobody has. I should take them back to Bert. That's the least I can do to make up for my foolishness.*

Waiting until the proprietor turned his back, Pascal snatched the dirt-filled bowl and fled to his car. "I've got you, Matilda," he made a little whinny of satisfaction, "and I'll get you back to your husband."

A giddiness swept over Pascal, sending his mind to twisted heights. He'd won! Bert would be proud of him for "rescuing"

Matilda from that sly undertaker. Had he not risked his life to claim Matilda's remains? If he hadn't been so brave, there was no telling who would have claimed her or what mischief might have befallen her.

That evening, Pascal found a roadside tavern and decided to celebrate his good fortune with a draft. He glanced nervously at the flower pot sitting beside him. "I'll leave you in the car, Matilda," he said. "A beer joint is no place for you. I'll be back."

He placed his hand on the pottery, frowning. "But what if someone steals you from me? What if that undertaker follows me and tries to get you back?"

With his head lowered, he tried to collect his thoughts. What would be best for Matilda? "I can't chance losing you again," he soughed. "I'd better take you in with me, even though I know you wouldn't be caught dead in a bar. I'm sorry, but you need me to protect you." He tottered into the taproom with the pot and carefully placed it on the counter in front of him.

As he swayed on the barstool, he tried to focus his blurry vision on the room-length mirror that covered the entire back wall. His head felt too large for his body and too heavy. He could hear the tinkling of glasses and the slapping of cards against a table, but the sounds seemed to crawl away. Somewhere someone plucked at a banjo with three monotonous chords that scraped across his nerves. He'd get some coffee first then go for something stronger.

He ordered black coffee, and while the bartender, a sloshy man with little dumplings under his eyes, went for it, he patted the earthen bowl. "Matilda," he whispered, "I'm glad I finally found you."

"What's in your crock, Mister?" A wiry man with a threadbare scalp and a volume twice his size pointed at the flower pot.

"None of your business," barked Pascal.

"Ah, ha. Growing something illegal, huh?"

"No!" Pascal didn't like the man's fishy stare.

"You're afraid to tell, aren't you?" taunted the patron.

"If you must know, it is Matilda. I am taking her back to her husband."

The man squinted at Pascal then hurriedly moved away. "Drunk as a skunk," he mumbled. "Thinks the old crock is his *girlfriend*!"

Word spread fast, and Pascal's clay pot became a tavern joke.

"Come on, boys," said one antagonist, "let's take a look at this purty thang. What color am them eyes?"

"Whooo-whooo!" whistled the leader of the pranksters. "Where on *earth* did he find her?"

"I wouldn't venture a guess, but a gal like that might do you some *dirt*," chirped another, setting off an avalanche of puns.

"Or *soil* your character."

"If I had a doll like that, my name would be *mud*."

"I'd get *grounded* for a year if my maw caught me with her."

"Yeah, I'd *dust* my hands of that'n."

Pascal sat sullen and silent. They didn't know what he knew; let them ridicule.

"It's probably her birthday, and this guy has her out on a special date," ribbed another. "Happy Birthday to you, Happy Birthday to you, Happy Birthday, dear Potsy, Happy Birthday to you!" The tipsy customer hiccoughed throughout the whole falsetto song.

"Tell you what," suggested a grinning onlooker, slapping his knee with glee, "since this is a special occasion, I think we should give the old gal something to drink. 'Tain't fair to drink in front of her and leave her thirsty."

"Yup," a buddy agreed, and so saying, he dumped half his tankard of beer into the dirt-filled bowl. "That's to you, Potsy, darling. And many more."

Pascal's face crimsoned, his temple swollen to a hard ridge. He jumped from the barstool, swinging his fists at the mockers. Pulsating with fury, he overturned the pot, chipping the edge and dumping sod on the counter.

Then seeing what he had done, he began to weep bitterly. "Oh, Matilda!" he blubbered. "I'm so sorry!" He tried to scoop the dirt back into the container. "I spilled some of you."

The gang moved in for more fun. "Come on, let's----"

"Boys!" shouted the bartender, slamming his ham-like hand on the table, rattling the mugs. The discordant mingling of laughter and shouts, the tramp of boots to music stopped abruptly. Silence dropped over the room like the lid on a trunk, leaving only a crackle of tension in the air. "Can't you see that the poor fellow is tetched in the head? I will not stand for you tormenting a helpless hapless! Say no more, or I'll throw all of you out!"

Pascal gathered the vessel into his arms and to the rhythm of cheap music reeled out of the saloon, sobbing aloud. "Matilda!" they heard him croon. "Oh, Matilda! I almost lost you!"

"Well, I never. . ." The ringmaster of the raggers gawked after him. "The simpleton was serious, wasn't he?"

Chapter Eleven

The Easter Lily

An hour after Pascal left the funeral home, the undertaker's wife returned from the beauty shoppe and decided to water her plant. She found it missing.

"Reuben," she said, "you moved my flower pot. Where did you put it? I sat it by the door so that it could get some sunlight."

"I didn't touch your plant, Willajean."

"Someone did. It's gone."

"You probably forgot where you put it. Plants don't get up and walk out."

"I'm not *that* forgetful. I put the pot there this morning before I went to get my hair done. It was one of the bulbs for my Easter lilies, and it was just ready to sprout."

"I plead innocent of any misdemeanor with regards to your beloved Easter bulb."

"Has anyone been in today?"

"No."

"This is a great enigma, Reuben."

"Oh, wait. There was a man in earlier asking about cremation. I remember now. An unusual fellow he was. Either he had passed some time at a barroom, or the book of his life lacked a few pages up front. He didn't quite make sense."

"What did he look like?"

"Rather ordinary. He wasn't bad-looking, but neither was he striking. He had curly, black hair, long sideburns and a short beard. His eyes were dark brown--and glazed. He drove up in a nice roadster. One fender was damaged."

"Do you suppose he stole my plant?"

"I don't know why anyone would want a jug of dirt, but----"

"Maybe he wanted something to put on a grave."

"That's possible. You might drive through the cemetery and find your seedling."

That night, Pascal hid his vehicle in a clump of sumac bushes and slept in an abandoned barn, a time-eaten building teetering toward complete decay, keeping the object of Willajean's dubiety beside him. He had cut his drinking short when he fled the tavern such that when he awoke the next morning, hunger had its full effect on his system. The gnawing in his stomach took him to the first greasy spoon cafe he could find.

He didn't wish to chance a repeat of the roadhouse scenario, yet he hesitated to leave the flower crock in the car. If he failed to get Matilda back to Bert safely, Bert would hold a vendetta against him forever. If he could return Bert's wife to him--in whatever form--Bert would exonerate him.

He sat parlaying, torn by frustration, while his need for food intensified. "I don't want to leave you, Matilda," he said, running a shaky hand around the pot, "but you shall not be hurt again."

The cafe was a small affair with a large front window. "I know what I'll do," he decided aloud. "I'll park close to the building and sit inside by the window where I can watch over you. If anyone comes near the car, I'll be out the door and beside you in a flash! You'll be warm here in the sunshine."

He got out and moved toward the eatery with a shaky,

braided walk. The table wasn't near enough to the window to suit him; he rearranged it, moving it to a spot where he could clearly see his car, and seated himself. Without taking his eyes from the vehicle, he ordered toast and milk.

As the cook toasted Pascal's bread, the one waitress, a hefty slob of a girl with unkempt hair, tried to make conversation with Pascal. Noticing that his attention was glued to the car, she made that her topic. "Nice car. Is it yours?"

"Yes."

"Is it new?"

"Yes."

"I never rode in a car."

"Hmmm."

"Could you come back when I get off work and take me for a ride? My name is Flossie."

"No, I'm leaving town."

"I could go with you."

"I already have someone riding with me."

"A girl?"

"Yes."

"Who is she?"

"Her name is Matilda."

"Lucky girl."

Two gentlemen came in, and the soubrettish Flossie moved away to take their order, chatting chummily with them, too.

"Has the riddle about the nameless girl been solved yet, Flossie?" one of them asked.

"Nope," Flossie said.

"What nameless girl?" the other gentleman asked with rude curiosity.

Something premonitory sliced like sharp steel through

Pascal's mind and struck his heart. He darted little stares at the men.

"A girl showed up at the hospital without identification. She had been injured in the head. Someone found her beside the road late one night. The authorities are beginning to suspect foul play. They're looking for a man named John Brown. They put a piece in the newspaper, but they haven't come up with any suspects. I expect when they do find the culprit, he'll get a stiff prison sentence."

"I'd say it would serve him right," said the friend. "How old was this little girl?"

"She was a grown woman. Early twenties, they think."

A flutter of panic paralyzed Pascal, thrusting him back into the unforgotten past. They were talking about Matilda! He had lied about his name to Vinnie Campbell, telling her he was John Brown. They were looking for him! And when they found him, he would be locked behind bars for years and years. Then how would Matilda's ashes get to Bert? They might take the flower pot from him and destroy it! He couldn't let that happen! His forehead beaded with perspiration.

He put his hands over his ears in an attempt to enclose his inner storm. What should he do? If he ran out of the cafe, the men might become suspicious and follow him. His eardrums pounded with the pressure of racing blood. "Flossie," he called, and the girl sloshed to his table. "I'm--I'm not feeling well. I'll take the toast with me, please." He laid a dime on the table and hurried out, forgetting his toast.

He gave the crank on the car's front grill a vicious yank, setting the machine to rollicking life, jumped in and left at the Tin Lizzy's maximum speed. He dared not look back.

He had not gone far before he realized he had left his food

behind. He was ravenously hungry, but he must get himself as far from Garden City as he could. Heading north, he didn't stop until he reached Belmead, forty miles away. He would get back to Bert eventually, but he couldn't chance traveling east on Highway 317, the route over which he had come with the living, breathing Matilda. Vinnie Campbell might see him and report him to the police.

How long ago had it been since the wreck? When he drank, his brain was filled with a whirring that dislodged his thoughts, shifting them around so that he couldn't trust the clock or the calendar. Had it been a week? two weeks? a month? He had lost track of the days as they wended through his bouts of drunkenness. Separate increments of time folded into one fabric.

Midday approached, and weak with hunger, Pascal found a boardinghouse that advertised home cooking. Farther removed now from the influence of liquor, he was able to think more rationally. He decided that he would ask the proprietor if he might bring his clay bowl inside with him out of the sun and wind. He would casually explain to her that it was a special gift for a special person and he wanted to safeguard it. That would make sense and allay suspicion. A surge of elation took hold of him. It would work!

The rich aroma from a wonderful soup larded the air. Pascal leaped from the car, his greed for action--and good food--building. The owner's smooth, oval face lit up with kindness, which seemed to be the native climate of her soul. "Bring in anything you need to," she encouraged, flinging the door wide. "Mi casa es su casa."

"Ma'am?"

"My house is your house."

Pascal bent to lift the flower pot from the passenger seat, and his world whirled, spinning itself into a funnel of terror. The bud of an Easter lily had pushed its way through the dirt.

"Matilda!" he cried, trembling from head to toe, "don't come up out of your ashes! I didn't mean to do it! Honest, I didn't. Go back! Go back! I'm taking you to Bert as fast as I can get there. Give me time." An unnamed wail came from his soul, a protest against nature's miracle.

The manager of the boardinghouse waited in the doorway like a large, framed picture. She saw Pascal put his hand to his heart as if he had taken a mortal blow. She was beside him in an instant. "My dear sir, what is the matter?"

"It's--she's--coming up." The words staggered out in whimpering agony.

She looked into his sunken face, a face that was pale and gaunt. There were shadows like bruises beneath his eyes. "Sir, I perceive that you have traveled so far without food that you have become quite disoriented from faintness. Here, hand me that plant. I will give it the most gentle care while you eat a nourishing meal." She took the container from his hands. "Now follow me, and eat as much as you possibly can. With renewed strength, you can take your lovely plant and proceed to your destination."

"Why--why is she--she coming up from the--the ashes?"

"Someone probably gave her a nice drink, and the sun----"

Pascal's stomach gave a heave. "Yes, yes. Someone gave her a drink."

"Eat, young man. The plant will take care of itself. It is *you* who needs care."

Pascal ate to his fill but not without the rancid taste of fear. He wanted to tell the kind proprietor that the bowl held Matilda's remains, but some foresight held him back. He'd like to let her know that Matilda, who would never have touched an alcoholic drink, now revolted againt the brew she had been given in the saloon. But would the lady understand?

Was it only last night that the guzzlers profaned Matilda?

He tightened his mind against the memories of it. Nothing had gone right all day; the day had been a thousand hours long.

The owner of the boardinghouse placed the pot in his hands as he left; she would not let him pay for his meal. She stood at the door and watched him drive out of sight, his face set deliberately, steadily on the road ahead. A hysterical sense of relief embraced her when he was gone. However, long after she was in bed waiting for sleep, his face etched itself on her thoughts. What was he running from?

Chapter Twelve

Surprise Visit

In small communities, no secret is sacred. Gossip travels from ear to tongue and tongue to ear like a tumbleweed blown by a West Texas wind.

Matilda's leaving occasioned stories in many versions, including full-blown fiction and unabridged myths. Mrs. Neuse, who had always been cursed with too much imagination, was willing to lean whichever way the tale-gale blew. Her tongue flapped like washing on a line. Any friendship with her was made with scandal and more of it. She enjoyed the interest the gossip called to herself, and she didn't take it kindly when the attention veered off in a different direction.

"Methinks the husband's friend was just a go-between," a neighbor surmised. "The girl was wild at the roots, and the boy helped her get away. It was all premeditated. She didn't want the responsibility of a husband and a baby, that's what I say. She's somewhere living like the devil."

"Might be so," agreed the landlady. "Her husband sure ain't grieving none. He gave the baby to his in-laws and is going right on with his life. He hasn't missed a beat. It might be that he was gladsome to be rid of her. It might be that *he* had someone else."

"I think she and that friend left on the train," said another.

"I dare say they're larking in California right now. That's where a lot of people go for pleasure. There's beaches and movies and worse."

"Wouldn't the ticket agent know?"

"Not if they falsified their names."

"Some allow it couldn't have been Mr. Conner's friend that she ran off with. She left in a fancy roadster, and Mr. Conner's friend was poor as a church mouse."

"She probably left with someone she met when she worked at that drugstore. A crew of telephone men were through here putting in lines, remember? Could have been one of them. Didn't you have a *hint* something was amiss, Mrs. Neuse?"

"Oh, yes!" The old lady tightened her thin lips. "I knew all the while that something was going on. All morning the day she left, I heard her scurrying around in her quarters. She was packing her luggage. I was in bed, but I heard her sneak in that night and pick up her gripsack about half an hour before her husband came in. Yep. Her wedlock was a short horse and soon curried. Along came the pied piper. And--get this--her husband put up a big front and pretended he didn't know she had left him!"

"You had the baby that night, right?"

"I did. Oh, she planned it well, all righty! They gave me two bits to keep him. Mr. Conner left the baby until the morning, and I went over in person the next day and made Mr. Conner 'fess up that his wife had bolted and wasn't coming back."

"With her husband's friend visiting so frequently and with her husband gone to school, there is no telling what happened."

"There must have been dry rot in the foundation of the marriage."

"The baby is the one I feel sorry for. It will have to live its lifetime with the shame and disgrace of a shameless mother!"

"Boys can handle abandonment better than girls can. Anyhow, that's Mrs. Gray's opinion." Mrs. Neuse liked to twist the meaning of people's words just enough to set them against one another.

"I disagree with Mrs. Gray----"

Many other such conversations, each more vicious than the one before, took place in Mrs. Neuse's sitting room. It was the incubator for evil communications.

To Bert, the days went by unpropitious and wrenched from their purpose. Life was a vacuum. How could everything be so different in such a short span of time? Like a clock that its owner forgot to wind, the house had stopped. No warm meals, no baby's laughter. Things like his socks got lost and stayed lost. The lamplight didn't seem as bright--and sometimes he didn't bother to light it. He listened for sounds that never came, one of those sounds being her voice.

Dogged determination goaded him on. His grades suffered, but he managed to pass his tests. The professors understood and gave him their finest support.

Mr. Davis came to offer him bigger and better opportunities to play for highbrow dances. Bert, he said, had made a name for himself at the Chalk Mountain Jamboree, and the door stood ajar for large financial gains. When Bert declined his offer, Mr. Davis raised his price to ten dollars an evening. "And you can have all the mad money that lands at your feet," he laughed.

"Thank you, Mr. Davis, but I won't be playing the fiddle again. Since I lost my wife, there is no music in my heart. I'll manage without the money."

No amount of persuasion on Mr. Davis' part could change Bert's mind. Saturday nights, the night most dancing took place, was reserved for a visit to Little Henry.

Bert wrote his mother that with the stress of finishing his last semester, he would not come home again until school was out. He hoped she would understand. When she got his letter, she made a quick decision to ride the train to Walnut Springs and surprise him with a visit. He had made the journey home faithfully each weekend for three years, and now it would only be fair for her to reciprocate. Anyone should be able to direct her to Mrs. Neuse's rental rooms. Bert had said he lived only a short distance from the college.

With her mind settled, Bert's mother rushed about and made her trip at once. As she descended the steps of the Pullman coach with her suitcase at Walnut Springs, she saw Bert at a distance, hurrying toward town. "Son!" she called out, and he turned around to see who called.

He paused. "It's your mother come for a weekend visit," she motioned to him. "What a streak of good fortune that you were passing this way. Now I won't have to inquire after your address. Where were you headed?"

He dare not tell her that he was going to see his child; she didn't know he had a son. His trip to Brazos Point would have to be postponed, and he would spend the weekend torn between the joy of seeing his mother and the longing to see his baby. Either concession was a miserable compromise.

It was fortunate for him that he had taken Henry's highchair --and all his things--to Sarah. Thanks be, he'd not be forced to break the news of his fatherhood to his mother until after graduation. And, luckily, he had stowed (and locked) Matilda's personal belongings in the slatted trunk out of sight.

"I was going to visit. . . some friends," he said, "but I can go later. Come along to my rooms. Here, let me carry your portmanteau."

Bert's mother knew instinctively that something was amiss.

Some unbridgeable chasm gaped between them. She felt hopelessly unsupplied with words for mending the elusive tear. She pried silently, constantly for answers. "You've lost weight," she mentioned. "Have I not sent enough money for food?"

"I have been studying hard, Mother. I've hardly taken the time to eat."

"I will cook for you while I am here."

"That sounds good." He pasted on a milk and water smile. The thought of missing his visit with Little Henry brought a consummate void.

She finally got around to asking the question Bert knew was coming and dreaded. "Where is Pascal?"

"I don't know, Mother. He. . . left."

"He lives here with you, doesn't he?"

"He hasn't lived with me for the last two years."

"But son! We promised Pascal's father that we would take care of him! You were quite young when your father died but not too young to remember that we were left homeless and in debt. Your father had mortgaged everything we had for the blacksmith shop, and then he was killed. Pascal's father, our neighbor, negotiated with the real estate company for our rent. Then when he was on his deathbed, he willed us the big house with the stipulation that we would care for his poor, orphaned Pascal. I made him a promise----"

"I did my best for Pascal, Mother, until he was eighteen years old."

"He is not of legal age until he is twenty-one."

"He makes false claims to be twenty-one now. I feel that our responsibility for him has ended. Two years ago, he began to drink----"

"Oh, no! Don't tell me! Where did I fail? Oh, I failed

Pascal's father!"

"You didn't fail. Pascal's real character has emerged. In his nature lay idleness and dishonesty. He has made his own choices, and they are not good ones, I'm afraid." Bert dropped the subject into a pool of silence.

The weekend dragged by with Bert almost strangling in his effort to keep silent about Pascal's knavery and his own agony. How could he tell his mother that his world would never be whole again? That there was in him another person he was protecting?

On Sunday afternoon, Hank Gibson knocked on the door. When Bert saw him, he held a warning finger to his lips. "Please come in, Mr. Gibson," he said with elaborate diffidence and courtesy. "And may I present my mother? She surprised me with a visit."

"I'm pleased to meet you, Mrs. Conner. I, uh, I stopped to see if you were well, Bert. We expected you out to the farm----" Hank stammered.

"I will visit next weekend if that will be convenient, Mr. Gibson. Please express my apologies to your wife if I misput her with my change of plans." His words suggested dismissal.

Hank left. The encounter, though short, left Bert feeling weary. It had been a close call.

As for Bert's mother, she felt as near to the core of some important issue as she had ever been, but whatever it was eluded her. "Who is this Mr. Gibson?" she asked.

"He's a farmer who befriended me. A father figure, I guess you could say."

"You've never mentioned him in any of your letters."

"No." His throat was thick and full. He hated his deception.

The frantic second lasted only that. His mother changed the subject. "Do you still play your fiddle, son?"

"I haven't played for a while. Really, I've done little more than sleep and go to school."

He was glad when she suddenly aborted that subject, too. "This apartment needs a good cleaning. Bachelors are not scrupulous housekeepers. I think I will stay over an extra day and scrub while you are in school tomorrow. I'll cook you up some food. You are studying too hard; you're not my old Mr. Pep anymore. I will be glad when school ends."

"So will I."

She stayed, and she cleaned. Something had her son distracted. What could it be?

This old trunk, she complained to herself, *takes up a lot of room. I daresay it belongs to Pascal.* An uncommon curiosity possessed her. Normally, she was not nosy. *I wonder what Pascal has stored here.*

With the help of a hairpin and a knifeblade, she managed to unlock the trunk. There, folded neatly, were Matilda's petticoats, bonnets, dresses, and stockings. On top of the lot lay a Bible.

So! Pascal had a woman in his life. He had taken a wife and moved out, deserting her son, neglecting his part of the living expenses. Pascal had always wanted to have his cake and to eat it, too.

Her son was lonely; that was his problem. Well! She'd fix that. Just let him get his education behind him, and there would be plenty of girls to vie for a handsome graduate's attention. She could think of several desirables now: Annabelle Preston, Lettie Briggs, Sharon Newman. . . . She would have some parties that would foster a festive atmosphere.

She picked up the Bible that lay atop the clothing, opened it and read the name on the flyleaf: *Matilda Gibson.* Pascal and Matilda. . . She closed and locked the trunk, satisfied with what she had learned.

When Bert returned from classes, his mother alluded to the trunk. "Is that Pascal's trunk?" she asked. "Will he be coming back for it?"

There was a long, heavy silence. Bert's hands closed into fists then opened. "Yes," he responded at length, trembling with temper, "I expect Pascal will come and pick up that trunk--someday."

Chapter Thirteen

The Diagnosis

Nurse Retha Bennis watched the mail for replies to her appeal for help in finding Mr. John Brown. She received only one letter. It was from a widow in Belton who had a son named Jonathan. Her son, the woman wrote, attended the Baylor University in Waco and was an upstanding citizen studying to be a lawyer. She had asked him to drop by the hospital and talk with the doctor.

When the young man came in, the doctor discounted him as a witness at once. He knew nothing of the accident, the girl, or the Campbells. He was polite and respectful, expressing his regrets that he was not able to be of assistance.

For the first week in Retha's home, Matilda sat quietly and did needlework while Retha worked her hospital shift, feeling adrift on an uncharted sea. Alone in the hush of the house, she had time to think. It bothered her immensely that she did not know who she was. Did she have a father? a mother? If so, why weren't they searching for her? Her past was nothing but a black and cold wall with no ladder for her to climb.

Sometimes feelings came over her that she could not shake, feelings of isolation and fear. Whatever she happened to be doing, a shadow could fall across her like a cloud crossing a field on a sunny day. She was cut in two, suspended between two worlds: the world of yesterday (of which she remembered nothing) and the uncertainty of tomorrow. A numbness emanated not from pain or grief or anger but from the nothingness that surrounded her. She couldn't bear the prospect of time with no meaning as the months rolled slowly by in the wake of days, each day a pattern of the others.

Vinnie Campbell came and took her to the scene of the accident. It proved to be a disappointing day for both of them. Matilda had no recall of the road, the ditch, or the fence.

Then one afternoon Retha returned to the sound of music. Matilda sat playing the pianola in the parlor.

"Linda!" she clapped. "That is beautiful! Have you always played?"

For a moment a candle burned behind Matilda's face; then over the light swept the shadow. "I don't know, Miss Bennis. I just sat down, and my fingers found the notes."

"What were you playing?"

"*Nearer My God to Thee*."

"Is that your favorite song?"

"No, my favorite song is *Amazing Grace*."

"How do you know that *Amazing Grace* is your favorite song?"

"I don't know how I know. I just know."

Retha sensed a stone of unrest within Matilda; it was especially noticeable at night when evening drew a canopy over the earth. The emptiness of spirit and will was not a good index for a person so young. The girl often had a haggard, unslept look. "Do you sleep well at night, Linda?" she quizzed.

"No, ma'am. Most nights I thrash and toss while sleep runs from me."

Retha made a mental note to mention this to the doctor. "I'm praying for you, Linda." She weighed her words with care. "God knows where you are and who you are. We must be patient while He works out His plan. Do you think it would help if you had a job?"

"I could try to work."

"There's an opening at the laundry. The hours are long, and the pay is minimum: ten cents an hour, ten hours a day."

"What would I be doing? Would it be simple?"

"Yes. It is general labor. Sorting clothes, working at the boilers, folding sheets----"

"I could do that!"

Matilda went to work Monday morning. Her face was pale, but it exposed none of her inner tumult. The day started with the smell of starch and hot cloth under the presses, and she gained confidence as she went along. However, by midafternoon after being on her feet for seven hours, she felt weak, nauseated, and dizzy. The supervisor suggested that she sit down for a few minutes. "You'll get used to the heat," he said. "For your first day, you are doing well."

The next day, he put her on a lighter job in a different room. Here a large group of women, a potpourri of busybodies, ironed and folded clean linens. Matilda's responsibility was to tag and label the linens for customer pickup.

The co-workers tried to draw Matilda into their discussions. "I hate living with my grandma," a girl called Belle complained. She was a headstrong lass with an unbridled tongue. "She believes that everything I do to have fun will lead me to eternal damnation. Take, for instance, my new beau. She thinks I ought to drop him because he swears. She has threatened to run him off when he comes to visit. What should I do?"

"Ask the new girl," someone suggested. "The rest of us are fresh out of answers."

"Linda, what do you think?" asked Belle.

"I--I don't know."

"He's a good dancer and easy on the eyes. If Grams sends him packing, I won't have anyone to two-step with on Saturday nights."

Dancing? For one instant of time, life teetered on the edge of a black pit for Matilda. The pit would swallow her forever once she fell in. It seemed that a hand had seized her by the throat and that she couldn't breathe. She reached for a table to steady herself.

"Are you all right, Linda?" asked Belle. "You're as white as death."

"I--I think so."

"We had this really great fiddler at the last dance----"

Matilda's world swam out of focus. Waves of terror rushed through every part of her being.

"You're sick, Linda!"

"Yes, I----"

"Sit down and put your head between your knees before you faint. Quick!"

"Maybe she's in a family way," an older woman volunteered.

"Are you, Linda?" the garrulous Belle pried.

"I'm not married. At least, I don't guess I am."

"She isn't making sense, girls," the older woman said. "Call the supervisor."

"No, please. I'll be fine in a minute," insisted Matilda. She had discovered that a smiling helplessness was her best protection. "I am a victim of amnesia."

"Is it catchin'?" Belle recoiled as if she had touched a hot coal. "I haven't had my shots."

"No. It is a loss of memory due to a head injury."

"You mean, you can't remember your past?"

"That's right. I was in an accident, and I can't remember anything that happened before the injury."

"Hey, I wish I had amnesia!" The ragged speaker gave a sardonic laugh. She had learned that misery could be removed only by making a joke of it. "I'd be glad to forget my drinking husband, the lame cow and my empty cupboard. I'll trade places with you, Miss."

The talk depressed Matilda. She confessed her inner struggle to Retha that night. "I don't like working there," she said. "The women are crude."

"It is likely that you have never worked in public before," Retha said. "We have to learn to take the good with the bad. Every type of work has its drawbacks, its hardships. It will smooth out."

But it didn't smooth out. Each day grew worse.

"Linda was probably one of those church-going goody-goodies in her other life," Belle taunted one day. "If I were you, Linda, I would make hay in this new life. You're too young and pretty to waste your time sitting home with an old maid nurse. You should go out and party. I can introduce you to some handsome critters."

Matilda flinched. The conversation made her uncomfortable and agitated. She wanted to be left alone to do her job.

By the end of the week, her feet were pitifully swollen. Her skin felt tight and hot, a size too small for her. "I think I am becoming ill," she told Retha. "I thought I was going to collapse today."

"There is a possibility that you have internal injuries of which we are not aware," the nurse said. "I will make an appointment for you to see the doctor. The swelling of those feet is not normal for a girl your age."

"Another doctor's appointment? But I already owe so much!"

"Your health is worth more than money, Linda. Even your face is gorged and flushed. The doctor will want to have a look at you."

After the doctor's examination, he had a private talk with the nurse. "I can't believe I let this 'problem' slip by me, Retha. Linda is carrying a child. My guess is that her gestation will be complete by early fall. I'll ask you to break the news to her; I think it would be better for a woman to do it."

Retha wore a shocked expression. "Doctor, do you think she might be a victim of--er----"

The doctor's eyebrows climbed and then descended slowly. "We have no answers, Nurse. Only more questions. Life does not excuse mistakes for whatever reason. But she has been cast on our hands, and we must care for her." He dropped his voice as he spoke; it held a strange commingling of compassion, fatigue and worry. "Get her a good tonic as she's a bit anemic."

"Should she quit work?"

"Let her work as long as she is able. Her mind needs the outlet."

"This complicates matters, doesn't it?"

"Yes. Find out if she wants to keep the child or put it up for adoption. I have several qualified applicants that would give her baby a good home. If we have no further clues to her identity by birthing time, I would recommend that she place it. If she should try to raise it herself, the child would suffer the stigma of being fatherless, and Linda would have an added burden on top of her amnesia. Frankly, in her condition, I don't think she can successfully handle motherhood."

Troubled, Miss Bennis took Matilda to the quiet of her sitting room to break the news. She tied back the curtains and fluffed the sofa pillows to posit normalcy. How could one buttress such a shock? "The doctor says you will have a baby in late August or early September, Linda."

"I will?" The question was a frightened and helpless note suspended somewhere in midair with no staff to support it. "I--I didn't know. But, of course, if that is what God wants, . . ."

"The doctor suggests that you start giving some thought to the future. There are childless couples who are financially secure who will take care of your medical bills and rear your child for you since you have no husband."

"You mean, give away *my child*?" Matilda, overwhelmed with the agony of her predicament, began to weep. The tears rent Retha's heart.

"You don't have to decide today, Linda." She put her arms around Matilda. "Pray and try to think what would be best. It may take a great deal of unselfishness and love for your baby to make the proper decision."

"What about my job?"

"The doctor says you may keep working as long as you feel able."

"With a child to support, I must work."

However, when the supervisor learned of Matilda's condition, he fired her immediately. "It isn't good for the reputation of my business to hire an unwed mother-to-be," was his vituperation. "We hire only women with the highest of morals."

Nor would any other business establishment hire Matilda. The prejudice she faced was the first awesome, agonizing realization that she could not hope to keep her child. How would she feed and clothe it if no one would hire her? Despair swept over her like an avalanche, leaving her heart hammered and sore. She gave a low wail that tapered off to a moan.

CHAPTER FOURTEEN

The Sacrifice

"Have they got aholt o' Bert yet?" Martha asked Sally.

"Yes, Mama, they brought him out of his school classes. The doctor thinks Little Henry may not live. Bert won't leave his side."

"What'd th' doctor say was th' matter with Little Henry?"

"It's an intestinal flux. They have a new name for it, but I can't pronounce it. The doctor says it is not uncommon in a child's second year of teething. The lining of the colon sheds itself off."

"Oh, landsy! That's what Sarey's first baby had, an' she's layin' in yon cemetery. That's what William's little Billy had when we found th' Taylors broke down at th' river an' God had Chester here to pull him through so poor, childless Nellie would have a chance at motherin'. . . ."

"The doctor is doing the best he can."

"I know, Sally-girl, I know. It's up to th' Father above. An' to thank if'n Little Henry up an' dies, Tilly won't even be here for his layin' away. We'll have to do all th' grievin' ourselves. Can you b'lieve Tilly's out livin' like th' imps an' her baby a-dyin'? Sin collects mighty high wages, I tell ye.

"Right now it might not make no difference to Tilly 'bout that little'un, but when she grows older, it'll be somethin' that so haints her she can't live with herself night nor day! She'll boot herself for her foolishness an' wish a million times she could undo it."

"And we'll have to do all the praying for Henry's healing, Mama. Bert isn't a praying man."

"If this don't humble him, I don't know what will. Mayhap it'll start him on thoughts of prayer. Sarey said his maw had been to see him."

"Yes. Last weekend."

"An' he didn't even bring her out here to see his child. He's still hidin' th' truth from her. When Hank went in t' see him, he bade him be quiet about it. I tell you, that's outright dishonesty, an' he's not without guilt himself. Th' Lord may be collectin' some pay for some wrongs. I don't know if He'll hear our petitions for Little Henry with so much mish-mash goin' on."

"I'm going over to Sarah's to see how the baby is doing."

"I wisht I was able to git out of this chair an' walk over there with ya. But I'd prob'ly do more good stayin' here----"

"And worrying."

"Why, certainly, Sally. Prayin' an' worryin' holds up each other's hands. Remember?"

Tilly, Tilly, Martha talked to her absent granddaughter, *they say you ran off with a man, but when I git down t' th' bone bottom of thinkin' on it, I can't b'lieve you really did that. You was a good girl. I want you to come back b'fore I lay in my pine box an' look me in th' eye an' tell me th' honest truth. How can a crippled up ole gran'ma like me really know th' truth? I jest have to go by what they tell me, an' thangs ain't always like you hear 'em.*

A midafternoon nap interrupted Martha's conversation with the unseen girl. The palaver bled over into her dreams. Matilda came and held Martha's hand, saying, "Don't believe them,

Grandma. I am innocent of any wrong. I love my husband and baby. I am pure."

The screen door, closing behind Sally, woke Martha. "I know you're innocent, lamb," she said aloud to the Matilda of her dreams.

"What did you say, Mama?" Sally asked.

"Nothin'. I was jest talkin' to little Tilly."

"Tilly?"

"Why, yes. She was here----" Martha chuckled. "I've been asleep, haven't I? I dreamt of Tilly. But, tell me, how is Little Henry?"

"Little Henry isn't any better, Mama. It seems that every breath he takes will be the last, but he fights on. Sarah wants me to call Chester. He's a specialist in children's ailments."

"By all means, Sally. Why didn't we think of that b'fore? He helped pull Billy through. There's th' horn. Don't waste no time. Call now."

"He's probably at work."

"Call his work. Central will help ye find him. Tell her it's an emergency. That's what them horns are for."

Two calls connected Sally to Chester, and he agreed to take the next train out of Austin. Hank met him at the depot. "Let me stop in to talk to Dr. Pyre," Chester said. "I want to know what I'm facing."

Hank waited in the wagon while Chester talked to the local practitioner. Chester came out shaking his head. "Sounds bad," he commented. "I need to talk to Matilda. We'll be fortunate to save her baby. How is she holding up?"

"Matilda, uh, isn't here. Sarah has had her little boy for more than a month."

"Where is Matilda?"

"We don't know."

"She just--left?"

"Yes."

"Why didn't Mama let Candice and me know?"

"It's been kind of embarrassing to your mother--the way Matilda left and all. We kept hoping she would return."

"That doesn't sound like Matilda, Hank, to just up and leave. She's a level-headed girl."

"Anyone can make a rash decision, but we felt sure she'd be home by now."

"Did she and Bert have a disagreement?"

"No. Bert didn't have a clue that she was leaving."

"And you've had no word from her in a *month*?"

"Not a word."

"What about Bert? How is he taking it?"

"Bert is a trooper. He hasn't left his son's side since Little Henry fell ill. He really loves the boy. With Matilda gone, I don't know how he can bear the loss of the child, too."

When Chester saw Little Henry, his worst fears were confirmed. He called Bert aside. "I'm afraid the child's only hope for survival lies with a large hospital. He has an intestinal infection that works swiftly with a death rate of fifty to ninety percent."

"What caused it?"

"Bacteria. *Vibrio comma.* It has a short incubation period, and dehydration is our greatest enemy. It not only begins quickly, it runs a fast course in small children. I need to get him to the hospital in Austin today."

"Do what you must to save him."

"Our chances hang on a vaccine. But I will be up front with you, Bert. It is expensive. As for me, I gladly offer my services without charge, but there will be considerable charge for serum."

"I'll pay it out as I can."

"The hospital may require an entrance fee."

"How much?"

"The normal deposit is ten dollars."

"Take him on, and tell them I'm on my way with the money."

Chester didn't take time to visit with Martha. "Tell Mama that this is a life or death matter, Sarah. I'll see her on the next trip." He wrapped Little Henry in a blanket and climbed back into the wagon. "Hurry, Hank," he urged. "There's only one more locomotive out today, and I have to be on that train."

After Chester left, Sarah walked to her mother's house. "With my grandson's life in the balances, I can't bear to be alone," she said. "My arms ache empty."

"I 'spect if th' youngster passes on, Bert's mother'll never know she had a gran'son. Kinda sad, ain't it?"

Sarah was distracted. "Can I spend the night here, Mama? Chester whispered that if the baby should die, he would call on your horn. I want to be here in case the call comes. Hank will come on over when he gets back from town. Bert is going to Austin after he gets the admission charge for the hospital. I figure he plans to borrow the money somewhere."

By morning the telephone had brought no message. It rang several times, bringing Sarah up with a start, but it wasn't Martha's ring. "They say no news is good news," Sally encouraged.

It was several hours before they learned the good news. Little Henry would live. It was a week before they learned of the great sacrifice Bert had made for his child. He had sold his violin, the instrument that had belonged to his father and his grandfather before that to pay for his son's medication.

"One good thang about that," quipped Martha, "he sure

won't be playin' at no more of them wicked dances!"

Chapter Fifteen

The Flower Pot

Pascal's great consternation grew with the sprouting of the Easter lily. True, the lily would have grown faster had it stayed in the mortuary under Willajean's watchful watering, but its green tongue collected enough moisture from the air for thriving survival.

His desperation to get "Matilda" to Bert became an obsession with Pascal. When he ran out of money for fuel, he siphoned gasoline from other vehicles to put in his roadster. He scavenged for food. But at last he managed to get back to Bosque County, back to Walnut Springs.

Bert had settled back into his school routine after his trip to Austin. His makeup work consumed every spare minute of his time; he studied tirelessly and with little sleep. The countdown of six more weeks until graduation created a hectic schedule that gave him neither the luxury of missing Matilda nor the satisfaction of despising Pascal. That would come later.

Mrs. Neuse had been over asking impertinent questions. Had he heard from Matilda? No, he told her, and he didn't care if he never heard from her. Was he going to remarry? She had someone in mind for him. No. He'd never trust a woman again. Would he be moving from the apartment when school was out? Yes. The sooner the better.

Every word Bert said to her was edited, amplified and mistranslated for the benefit of the "sewing bees" who came to quilt on the quilting frame dangling from the ceiling of Mrs. Neuse's living room. "His mother visited him recently," Mrs. Neuse reported. "She's a widow lady. And do you know what Mr. Conner had the nerve to do? He invited Mr. Gibson over to meet her. And Mr. Gibson a married man!"

"Does he still fiddle for dances?"

"No. He sold his fiddle. Talk about irresponsible! He sold that priceless instrument to a peddler who came through drumming knickknacks. Sold it for *ten dollars*. Why, it was worth five-fold that much! I've seen it; I know."

"I'd say he didn't sell it, he gave it away."

"I heard his little boy nigh died of dysentery," goaded a spiritual sister.

"Oh, that was just a bid for sympathy," scorned the landlady. "So's I wouldn't raise his rent like I was planning on doing. I think his kid wasn't even sick. I think Mr. Conner went to Austin to see some lady friend." And so the yarns unraveled.

Mrs. Neuse was looking out the window, minding everyone's business but her own when Pascal arrived to make his amends. A belated cool spell had blown in, and when she put her nose against the windowpane, her breath steamed the glass. She backed her face away with the speed of a roadrunner, wiping at the window with the tail of the curtain to remove the vapor and see the better. Ah, here was a juicy morsel to report at the next meeting of the rumormongers!

Pascal lurched his way to the door, the ghost of a smile loitering on his lips. He'd made it! His relief was as exaggerated as his earlier anxiety. Mrs. Neuse heard him pound on the door, saw the door open, and then the drama was lost to her. She put her ear against the wall but could hear nothing.

Inside, Pascal shoved the flower pot toward Bert. He was wild-eyed and excited. "Here she is, Bert. I brought her back to you! She has been so anxious to get here, she tried to rise right up out of her ashes. . . ."

Bert beat back a dangerous seizure of animosity. He had no desire to be thrust back into the painful past. "Pascal," he said, his face graven with scorn, "I want nothing more to do with you. I tried to befriend you, and you betrayed me. My wife ran off with you--and you can *keep* her." He clasped his hands behind his back, refusing the clay pot Pascal held out to him. Only the glow of his smoldering eyes revealed the volcanic emotions building to an explosion. "Please leave."

Silent tears trickled down Pascal's face, a face lumped with distress. "Matilda didn't run off with me, Bert. Matilda didn't do anything wrong; she is innocent. Lay all the blame upon me. I was drinking, and I----"

Bert motioned Pascal to a chair. "Sit down and talk fast before I turn you into sausage."

"Please, Bert----" Pascal's misery enveloped the room.

"Talk!"

The story came out in an thick rush, an almost whispering sound composed of regret, contrition and self-accusation. "I told her a lie to get her away from the dance that night. I told her that Little Henry was ill and she was needed at home. Then when I got her in the car, I headed west. She begged me to stop to let her out. She wanted to walk home, to walk back to you. I kept drinking, and she became frightened and would have jumped from the moving vehicle if I hadn't caught her by the arm. When I reached for her, I lost control of the car. It spun about and hit a fencepost. The impact threw Matilda against something and knocked her out.

"I took her to the nearest farmhouse, where the lady promised to care for her. That's the last time I saw Matilda."

"You left her with strangers?"

"They did not invite me to stay. I learned the next day that she had died."

"Matilda. . . dead?"

"Yes. Oh, Bert, I am so sorry!"

"And I was not notified of her death?"

"They didn't know who she was. She was unconscious."

"You didn't tell anyone who she was?"

"I was trying to protect her reputation, Bert. I had already decided--before the accident--to get her back to you quietly so your landlady wouldn't smut her name. Everything I did was an effort to right my wrong."

"Pascal, you've been a dolt all your life!"

"Yes, I have, Bert. I've been an idiot. I don't know why you put up with me. I've always admired you, envied you. You've had what should have been mine--my father's house, a college education, and then a beautiful wife. That's why I had the notion to take Matilda. I saw her first; I wanted her first. When I drank, I convinced myself that life wasn't fair to me, that you weren't fair to me. I was wrong-headed. I'm the master of my own fate. I killed Matilda, Bert, but here she is." Pascal sat the pot he'd been holding on the table. His voice was like a knife cutting without mercy. "I thought you'd be proud of me for getting her back to you, and I had hoped that you would forgive me."

Bert, confused and lost in a labyrinth of half-formed thoughts, sat motionless. The potted plant was from Matilda's grave, of course. Pascal, small-minded Pascal with his misshapen spirit, thought that the offering of a funeral flower would sponge away all the grief he had caused.

Too well, Bert knew Pascal's personality when he was drinking. He considered himself the most important, most interesting person in the world. No arm was stronger than his, no mind more brilliant. And he thirsted for command. When he was full of whiskey, he was empty of sense. How many times had he forgiven Pascal in the past, laying Pascal's debts to the demon of alcohol? But Pascal had gone too far this time; he had crossed the line into the unforgivable.

A quiet mockery pervaded Bert's voice. "So you were privileged to attend my wife's funeral, and I wasn't."

"No. There was no funeral. I picked her up," he gestured toward the lily, "at the mortuary."

"And I'll never know where she was buried."

"That's why I brought her here to you." Pascal's face was greasy with tears of contrition. "Please forgive me, Bert. *Please* forgive me."

Bert was too harrowed to hear more. "I believe what you are saying, Pascal. I believe my wife is dead, but forgiveness is another matter." He felt wretchedly sorry for Pascal, but just now, a bitter aftertaste of white-hot rage outweighed all else in the contradictory jumble of emotions. He needed time for mental remustering. "Go away and let me sort things out."

"I'll be your servant forever, Bert! I'll spend the rest of my life making it up to you about Matilda!"

"Go, Pascal!" Bert's voice was firm, final, his eyes hostile and intent. He bit down hard on his back teeth.

"I'm--I'm hungry, Bert. I haven't had a bite of food since the day before yesterday. I was trying to get her here. Do you have two bits I can borrow?"

Years of habit overrode Bert's malice. His hand, without consulting his mind, reached into his pocket and dropped a coin into

Pascal's dirty, outstretched hand. "See that you buy food and not drink!" he thundered.

Suddenly, all the ravages of guilt were wiped away, and supposing himself absolved, Pascal's eyes became bright. "Thank you, Bert. I'll make it up to you--starting tomorrow."

Bert slammed the door against the sight of Pascal lest he transmit his fury into aggression.

CHAPTER SIXTEEN

Forgiveness?

The initial shock of Pascal's revelation passed, leaving a hard reality colder than a winter wind. The grief sank deep inside Bert and hit his stomach at its pit. The day had the quality of a nightmare.

Only for brief moments would Bert let his mind think of Matilda, like running his eyes across the distant horizon. He remembered small things she'd said and done, things he had taken for granted. She had been a good wife and mother, giving much and asking little. He found a very small comfort in the knowledge that she did not suffer; Pascal said she lost consciousness at the time of the accident and never regained it.

The one request she had made, just hours before she left, he had spurned. She asked him to play some hymn he did not know. He could have at least tried; he could have asked her to hum the tune for him, and he could have picked it up from there. This was but the first of the regrets that came to torment him.

His sense of outrage toward Pascal grew; Pascal was a thief. Hadn't the Mr. Spratt said Pascal took the roadster without pay? And now he had robbed Bert Conner of a wife. It was the ultimate loss--the one unacceptable, unbearable loss he's never allowed himself to think on. Pascal had robbed a small boy of a mother. He had robbed Hank and Sarah Gibson of a daughter. He had robbed Martha Harris of a granddaughter. And he expected a flower pot and a paltry "I'm sorry" to atone for all his thievery!

Bert lay in bed and could not sleep; the cold crept in around the door, but he did not care. What mattered? His heart was encased in pain, and he concurred with the great philosopher who said: *For small griefs you cry aloud, but big griefs must be borne inside.* How true that was!

At twenty-four and already a widower with a son to nuture, he felt himself in some fashion ageless. His ambitions for happiness had disappeared as suddenly and completely as the flame of an extinguished candle.

He would have to break the tragic news to Matilda's family. That brought a whole new cycle of dread. He was equipped with such scanty details. He should have pressed Pascal for more.

A great consternation caused him to bolt upright. Pascal had revealed nothing! Where did the accident happen? Who was the lady who cared for Matilda until she died? Where did Pascal get the flower pot? There was no way to follow up Pascal's story. The rascal! He'd find him and choke the whole story out of him! Then he'd go to the woman and learn where Matilda's body lay.

He thrashed all night, tossing his bed into rabid disorder. By morning his eyes stung from lack of sleep, but he had a floorplan. The first order of business was to shake some solid information out of Pascal. Matilda was dead; he had no doubts. He could tell when Pascal was inventing, and this time he wasn't. The roadster's crumpled fender gave witness to an accident. Bert just needed more facts. He followed his thoughts to the door.

Mrs. Neuse was standing there, knock-ready. When Bert strode out, she stepped back, her fist still raised.

"Well, Mr. Conner," she babbled, "I was just coming to

check on you. You've been mighty quiet these last few days, I must say."

"I've been studying, Mrs. Neuse. And minding my own business."

"Oh, I'm sure of that," she forged on. "I saw that you had company yesterday afternoon. Your friend came by. Had he any word of Matilda?"

"Yes, he did." The words were bitter, subtly venomous. "I have been informed that my wife was killed in an automobile accident last month."

"And how is it that you have only just now heard about it?"

Bert didn't make a practice of lying, but he was tempted to do so now. "She had no identification on her, and the authorities had no way of tracing her family."

"Then she went without your permission on this, ah, er, journey?"

"Matilda was an adult. She didn't have to ask me when and where she could go. The opportunity for the trip came unexpectedly." Bert kicked himself for bothering with excuses for the intrusive woman standing before him. He should send her to her rooms with no explanation.

"And I suppose your friend brought you the bad news?"

"He did."

She gave a snorting laugh. "And you believe him, do you?"

"I do."

"What a fool you are, Mr. Conner. After all the lies he has told you, all the money he has filched from you, and all the booze he has consumed----"

"I know Pascal well enough to know that he would not lie about so serious a matter as death, ma'am."

"Oh, he wouldn't? I think he would say anything to save

face. Tell me, have you anyone's word but his? Can he substantiate his story with concrete facts? Why did he wait so long to inform you, pray tell? I smell something fermenting under the floor of the story."

Bert lifted a critical gaze to the sky. His nose nibbled the air. "I believe the sky is promising rain, and I have an urgent errand to take care of in connection with my precious wife's death," he said, tight-lipped and dry-eyed. He stepped around her and hurried away, his face a mask of pent fury.

Pascal had lived in Mr. Hunter's milk shed for two years. The elderly gentleman, who had long since committed his own sons to the earth, let Pascal inhabit the shack free of charge. He had, in fact, furnished the makeshift room with a few delapidated furnishings, and his good wife had crocheted rag rugs for the dirt floor. It was about a mile from town, but today Bert didn't mind the walk. If he walked fast enough, perhaps he could outdistance the things he only dimly understood, only half absorbed because Matilda was gone and nothing else mattered.

It had been easier to be angry with her than it now was to yearn for her nearness. To know that she had been taken against her will and that she had died begging Pascal to return her to her family was a thought too awful to contemplate.

Bert's trot turned to a mad run as if he would escape the thoughts that pursued him. Burning pangs throbbed in every fiber of his muscles. He must flee some foe deep in his mind. He ran faster and faster. If he slacked, the enemy of memory would catch him. On and on he sped, urging his legs to a greater pace. His strength came from the poison that ran in his veins.

Pascal's roadster came into sight, its crushed fender obtrusively in view. Bert slowed, his breath bursting from his lungs in blasts. He wished there was some way to prepare himself for another encounter with Pascal. The closer he got to the shanty, the more effort his steps cost him. How would he handle the matter? Would he be able to restrain the urge for vengeance?

Bert knocked but got no answer. He knocked again, louder. Then he pounded. And called.

Finally, he tried the door. It was unlocked. When he opened it, a cloud of choking smoke curled about his head, making him cough and sputter. He couldn't see for the fog. Throwing the door open wide, he first stepped aside so that the room might air out.

Dimly, as the atmosphere cleared, he saw Pascal on the cot, a bottle clutched in his hand. Seeing that a rag rug smoldered, Bert drug it outside and fanned away the smoke, bringing relief from the dense fumes.

"Pascal!" he barked, but Pascal did not respond. He went to the cot to shake the man awake.

It was then he realized that Pascal was dead, a victim of smoke inhalation. He had obviously tried to start a fire and, in his drunken stupor, dropped a match onto the mat. The smoke had sent him to his destination beyond.

I told him not to spend that half dollar on liquor, Bert rued, more angry with Pascal as a corpse than alive. *Now I will never learn the details of Matilda's passing.*

It would be left to him to arrange for Pascal's burial and to return the car to its owner. On top of all that chafed his mind, this added onus seemed too much. Should he contact his mother? After a brief deliberation, he decided against it. He would tighten his belt and absorb the financial burden as best he could.

He returned to his apartment more slowly and with a greater weight on his heart than when he came. It would take fierce grit to finish the last weeks of his education. But do it he would. He would do it for his son. And for Matilda.

Back in his room, he watered the thirsty plant, somehow equating it with a likeness of Matilda, white and pure. Her face came before him, so clear and courageous that he could not see around it.

Then he thought of the trunk that housed her clothes. His mother-in-law would want that. He might keep an item or two as keepsakes, but he'd return the rest. He would keep the portrait.

He unlocked the chest and found Matilda's Bible on top of the garments. Matilda had loved the Book. He was a stranger to it, but suddenly it had a magnetic appeal to him. Lifting it reverently from its nesting place, he idly began turning pages. As he did, his life felt less futile; Matilda seemed closer.

He came to a verse that she had marked and read it: *But if ye forgive not men their trespasses, neither will your Father forgive your trespasses.*

Chapter Seventeen

Martha's Plan

When Sally came through the front door, Martha knew that something was wrong. It wasn't only the look on the face of her youngest; it was a forewarning. Like a boulder, a dark presentiment weighted down her breast. She braced herself for the new unknown.

"What is it, Sally?"

"Mama," Sally's voice was strained and thin, "we have bad news."

"I knowed it." There was a taut silence; unspoken words crowded the room. Martha watched as Sally turned her face deliberately away.

With measured effort, Martha pushed herself forward in the horsehair chair. "Tell it, Sally. It is Baby Henry?" Poised on the chair's edge, she looked like a great, rundown mansion, sagging and worn but with a lingering air of grandeur.

"No, it's Matilda." Sally struggled to find the words to tell the unspeakable. There was no easy way.

"I was afeared o' that."

"She's--she's dead."

She's dead. Two words can wrench th' heart t' breakin', burst all th' limits of feelin', Martha thought. *Hope is like a brittle shell. Words can shatter it.* Martha Harris had faced death with a son, a grandchild and a husband. And now, Matilda. *She's dead. . . .* The sound roared in her ears.

Once Martha made herself believe that if she prayed passionately enough, she could hold her loved ones in life--and that if her prayer wearied, they might slip away. She would pray and pray, daring not sleep lest she lose her hold. Now, with her threescore and ten almost spent, she conceded that God monitored the exit of all souls and that all her nattering could not stay His call.

Her fingertips came together, forming a crooked steeple. A spasm of distress twisted her mouth. "Tell me all about it, Sally. There's nothin' worser than th' unknown."

"Thank God, it wasn't as we thought, Mama. She didn't run away with a man. She didn't purposely leave her husband and baby. She was taken against her will----"

"Didn't I tell you so all along, Sally? Didn't I tell you she was kidnapped? Nobody would listen nor b'lieve me."

"Yes, Mama. You are usually right."

"Who stole her?"

"Bert's friend."

"Some friend!"

"It was a jilted lover sort of thing. This man had wanted to marry Matilda, and Bert got her. He took her for spite."

"How did he ever lure her away from her home without Little Henry? Did he tie her up an' drag her away?"

"According to Sarah's understanding, Matilda had gone somewhere on a visit with Bert while the landlady watched Henry. The 'friend' came where she was and convinced Matilda that her baby was ill and she was needed at home. Naturally, Matilda went with him, thinking of nothing but Little Henry. The man was drinking."

"Where was Bert?"

"I suppose he had gone somewhere with the gentleman he was visiting. Mayhap to the field. I really don't know."

"Go on with th' story an' don't mind my interruptin', Sally. I jest want t' straighten th' covers in my mind. You know how I never liked th' covers wrinkled up."

"I know, Mama. It's--it's hard for us all."

"Tell some more."

"Bert doesn't know where the friend took Matilda; only that it was somewhere out west. When Matilda realized what was happening, she tried to jump out."

"Oh, landsy, this is gonna be too much for my old heart t' take, Sally! Each tragedy multiplies my years. Did th' jump kill her, or did th' horses trample her to death?"

"You're getting ahead of me. They were in a horseless carriage."

"An' it runned over my Tilly! That's all them machines are good for, t' hurt people! I knowed these modern inventions was of th' devil, even if William does have one an' I rid in it once to Fort Worth. Those conglomerations are worser than spooked horses. You can't stop a horseless by sayin' 'Whoa.' Horses haven't much brains, but machines don't have *none*."

"When the driver saw that Matilda was going to leave the vehicle, he put it in a ditch and hit a fencepost. Matilda's head struck the window, and she died from the blow to her head."

"How has all this been found out after all this time, Sally?"

"Bert's friend came back and confessed. He brought Bert a vase of flowers from her grave."

"Sally, this is th' saddest sad of all, not having a grave nearby! If we could've buried Tilly here, that would have been some comfort to Sarey. Little Henry would've known his ma was there with his great-gran'pa, Henry Harris. Tilly wouldn'd'a been lonesome in th' earth in some far country." Martha stopped to wipe her tears and blow her nose. "Where was she laid t' rest, an' who spoke her into heaven?"

"Bert doesn't know."

"Why didn't he ask?"

"He was berattled when he got the news. It was such a shock and so different from what he--we all--thought that he didn't get proper information."

"He could throttle th' two-faced friend an' git it yet, couldn't he?"

"No."

"Why not?"

"Remember Hank telling us of a man who burned up in Mr. Hunter's milk shed?"

"Yes."

"That was Bert's friend, the one who took Matilda away."

"It was?"

"Now there's no way to find out anything about Matilda's funeral, and that is grieving Bert worse than anything else."

"Oh, th' poor, poor boy!"

"Sarah says he is nigh beside himself."

"Then Sarey will have t' raise Little Henry."

"Bert says he is going to raise the boy himself. As soon as he finishes school, he plans to take Little Henry away with him."

Martha groaned. "I think that's worser news than Tilly's death. As young as Bert is, he'll be bound to take him another wife. Like as not, we'll lose track of Little Henry forever. An' our circle up in heaven will be broken by a missin' piece. Sometimes I'm glad yore pa didn't live t' witness these miserable heartaches. He's restin', the lucky bird, whilst I'm totin' all th' load!"

"Sarah was afraid Bert wouldn't continue to the end of school, but he explained to Hank that he must finish his education so he can make a good living for his son. Hank says Bert is a good man except for his lack of religion."

Martha's eyes took on a distant look. "I was thinkin'." The sentence ended.

"Yes?"

"Is Sarey grievin' bad, Sally?"

"Yes, Mama, she's having a hard time. She says there's no pain on earth like the pain of losing one's child. There's a victory, too, though. She is relieved to learn that Matilda didn't run off with another man voluntarily."

"Th' death of a child is life's hardest blow. All th' heart's cryin' an' head agony from my Robert's death comes back to remind me when I think on puttin' a young'un in th' ground. It's like you bury a part o' yourself. This makes two for Sarey. An' what's so bad is that it amounts t' both of her daughters. There's no girls left for her. Boys are bad to give up, but I'm thinkin' girls would be harder. They're weaker an' most often closer t' their mother. Why, Sally, if'n I'd had t' give you up when yer baby buggy most nigh caught on fire from th' warshpot coals, I'd'a lost my mind forever. I tried till little crippled Effie died to repay her for rescuin' you, but I never could've if'n she'd'a lived to be a hunderd."

"I wish there was something we could do to help Bert."

"I wish he knew Jesus. That would be a comfort. I don't know what a'body does at a time like this without Him."

"Bert seems lonely. Hank says his father died when he was quite small."

Martha lurched forward. "Sally! I have an idee. A grand idee!"

"Is it a workable plan, Mama?"

"I know somethin' grand we could do for Bert an' Sarey an' Little Henry an' all of us'ns."

"Speak it."

"We could have a memorial service for Tilly right here at our own community church. Matthew could direct it."

"Yes. All the family would want to come."

"Yes, yes! We could have it th' same weekend as th' Harris reunion. We still have time t' get word to ever'body, even t' Joseph an' Amy in th' Territory----"

"It's New Mexico now."

"They could come by train. I don't s'pose there's anybody that couldn't get here, do you? Dessie will be off from her teachin' for Easter. Alan an' Chester can take a leave. They're not far away down there in Austin. Arthur an' Lucy can come along from The Gap, too. Matthew lives right here in Bosque County, an' William an' Nellie over at Cleburne. It would be like th' funeral we didn't get to go to. We could bring flowers an' sing songs an' pray."

"That is a beautiful suggestion, Mama. I think it would bring some peace to everybody. We'll want to have someone sing *Amazing Grace* because that was Matilda's favorite hymn."

"Tilly was our best singer. She had th' most wondrous voice, but yours is next best, Sally, so I think you ought t' be th' one that sings for Tilly's special gone-away service."

"Matthew's Pauline could play the pump organ."

"We could put up a marker for Tilly in th' Harris plot at th' cemetery an' put a big wreath on it. In body she wouldn't be there, but in spirit she would. She'd *want* us to do this for her."

"And I think Sarah would be glad for a service to remember Matilda."

"Jest plannin' it takes away some of th' crush. Can you git

letters out to ever'body right away, Sally?"

"I'll talk to Sarah and Bert first; then if it is agreeable with them, we'll get the word out to everyone immediately."

Sally talked to Sarah about a memorial service. Sarah talked to Hank, and Hank talked to Bert.

"I'm not a religious man, Hank," Bert said, "but if this is what the family wishes to do, I will be there. Like the rest of you, I missed the funeral. I find that leaves something unfinished for me."

"Matilda loved singing and music. Would you object to Sally's singing Matilda's favorite song?"

"Do what you think best. It will not only be a memory for you and her mother, but it will be a memory for me and my son. Wherever life takes me, I shall never forget--or be able to replace--your daughter, my Matilda."

Chapter Eighteen

Uncertainties

Bound in her cocoon of rejection, Matilda's whole being seethed with the emotional storm that shook her world, beating against her exhausted spirit and feverish brain. She grappled at problems that slipped away like minnows. Perhaps if she could sleep, the pieces would shift and form a pattern.

She had not been able to find employment anywhere; when her condition was disclosed, the interview was over. She was at the mercies of the nurse for her daily bread.

Her greatest torments were her own uncertainties that lurked in the clotted blackness of her mind. If only there was something to relate to something else and provide a focus for her thoughts! Was there a good man somewhere worrying about his unborn child, or was she an unprincipled woman? Should she feel shame? How could she be besmirched by sin and yet feel God so near? Only Retha Bennis believed in her. And maybe the doctor, but he wanted her to give up her child. That would be the hardest thing any mother could do.

At her next appointment, the doctor pressed yet farther. "Linda," he said, "I know that parting with your child will be difficult. It will take love in the highest degree on your part to give up your baby for adoption, but in your condition, I would strongly advise it. Who knows what turn your head injury may take in the future?

"Sometimes there are delayed complications such as seizures or bouts of blinding headaches. Your incapacities include a physical and emotional aspect. You are also financially disadvantaged. Please consider an adoptive family for your infant."

Matilda wrestled with the idea, praying and agonizing over it. The child, whatever the circumstances of its origin, was a part of her. Would it feel that its mother had abandoned it if she gave it away? Would she wonder about it, yearn for it until her earthly span was over?

Then the doctor arranged for Matilda to meet a woman who was frantic to adopt a child. "Linda, I want you to talk to this lady, spend the day with her. I don't usually do things this way, but it might help you with your decision," he said. "Yours is an unusual case."

Matilda shrank from the meeting, feeling poorly equipped and unready to face her problem. "We have plenty of time," she argued.

"That is why I want you to meet Mrs. Goldfinch," he said. "So that you will have adequate time to adjust to your decision, to do what is best for everyone concerned. Babies are sometimes early, and we don't know exactly when this one plans to arrive. Mrs. Goldfinch is the most suitable candidate I have ever had for adoption."

Mrs. Goldfinch came to retrieve Matilda in a satin upholstered touring coach driven by a trained chauffeur. She handed Matilda a lace parasol to walk from the porch to the vehicle. "I'm Abby Goldfinch," she announced. "The doctor thought we would do well to become acquainted since I am the one who will be adopting your new baby."

"I'm not sure----" A protest trembled on Matilda's lips.

"Of course, in a sense, you might say I will just be caring for it for you because you are not able."

"Oh, I thought----"

"I would make some stipulations, though. I would ask that you not interfere with the rearing of him or her. You would be able to see the child now and then at concerts or the theatre, or you could attend school functions. Anonymously, to be sure. Then when he or she is of age, we will let the choice of your exposure be left to him or her. Isn't that fair enough?

"I have no doubts that my husband and I will be such superb parents that by the time our child reaches maturity, we will have no reason to be jealous of a birth mother who has been unknown for all those years. I feel that we are being very generous. Most unwed mothers never know who gets their babies."

"But I don't even know----"

"We are well set. My husband is a cattle baron and has made a fortune for himself. I inherited a large sum from my forebears. Money is quite important in early childhood. If this baby should turn out to be a girl, she will have dancing lessons, music lessons, figure skating lessons, instructions in the opera and the fine arts.

"She will be sent to the finest finishing school anywhere and make her debut into society properly. Oh, but you will be proud when you see her picture in the newspaper commanding a place on the social page! If it happens to be a boy, he will enjoy the best educational opportunities--my husband prefers a military academy--and he will have riding lessons as well as driving sessions. He will also be involved in sports. He will fall heir to a large estate."

"What--what about church?"

The little circles of rouge on Mrs. Goldfinch's cheeks, like red quarters, moved up and down when she smiled. "Oh, my dear! We belong to the biggest church in town! My husband is on the Board of Finances. Why, they could hardly operate without our obese offerings! My husband is on the committee that tells the pastor when to come and when to go. He even helps set the parson's salary!"

"Salary?"

"The pay."

"Oh."

"We don't miss a business meeting. I'm on the sponsor list for all the socials and dinners. You would be welcome to attend our church although, of course, I wouldn't want it to be noticeable that you give our baby inordinate attention. But you could take a glance along with everyone else. That would be a good, nonobtrusive place of contact for you to consider."

"Are you filled with the Spirit?"

"Spirits? No, you don't have to worry about that, my dear. We don't drink in excess. We only imbibe at social functions where it would be impolite to refuse."

When they reached Mrs. Goldfinch's house, a sprawling mansion that exacted a whole city block, the driver helped Matilda from the car, and a butler met them at the door. Mrs. Goldfinch took Matilda to the parlor, gestured toward a leather chair, and rang for tea. "We'll take a tour of the place after we have had refreshments," she said.

The cool of the house fell over Matilda, fragrant with furniture polish and fresh flowers. It spread before her, massive, silken, luxurious in a profusion of bookshelves, andirons and lampshades. But the more she saw and heard, the more disconcerted she became. She couldn't hope to furnish a child with such a future, but what if her baby would rather have his own mother's love than all the finery?

The house had two stories and dormer rooms above that. "This will be the nursery," declared Mrs. Goldfinch, opening the door to a massive room on the second floor. There was yellow patterned wallpaper on the walls, a yellow spread on the bed, and a lamp with a yellow shade. The windows were cosseted with silk lambrequins. "We will have a full-time, live-in nanny and private tutors. Our bedroom is right next door."

My baby will sleep in a bed in this room. The unbidden thought choked Matilda.

They went outside. The hothouse, the rose garden, the pampered lawn added to the overwhelming distress that threatened to suffocate Matilda. What had she to offer against all this plenty? She wished to see no more. She didn't want to view the ponies in the corral, the goldfish ponds, or the servants' quarters. She wanted to go back to her small bedroom at Retha's and think. Her head felt light and her stomach queasy. A dragging weariness came over her, reminding her that she had slept little. Confusion writhed in her mind like a snake weaving its ugly head to demand her notice.

Mrs. Goldfinch noticed that she was losing Matilda's attention. She could not afford to brew an antagonism. She grabbed the girl's hand and talked fast. "As you see, dear, we are well prepared to provide magnanimously for the child you bring us."

"Please," Matilda murmured, taking a deep breath in an attempt to calm herself, "I'd like to go back now. I'm--I'm not feeling well."

"Oh, I hope----" worried Mrs. Goldfinch. "I mean, there's nothing wrong, is there? Nothing that would jeopardize the--the child?"

"I'm very tired," Matilda said. "I didn't rest well last evening."

"Yes, certainly. I will call for the car."

They were exiting the mansion when Mr. Goldfinch rode up. He was a tall, impressive man with a surprisingly soft voice. When his wife introduced him to Matilda, he seemed pleased.

"Linda Brown!" he smiled. "Somehow you don't fit the picture I had conjured up in my mind. You are a most charming and lovely lady. Why, you could pass for a genuine aristocrat." He winked.

"We have been discussing the baby," Mrs. Goldfinch interjected. "I've been showing her what we have to offer a child."

"Abby wants a girl," Mr. Goldfinch explained, "so she can name her Abigail for herself and make her a regular socialite. But I want a son to carry on my name when I'm gone."

Matilda could not discipline the emotion out of her face. The pain in her eyes touched Mr. Goldfinch. "You must not worry, Miss Brown. We shall provide well for you, paying all your medical bills. And now that I have met you and recognize what a refined lady you are, I feel that I can offer you a good job as a secretary for my cattle company in South Texas--after the baby is born, that is. We want you here until then so that Abby may check on you now and then to see that all is well. Is there anything you need? Clothing? Hosiery? Shoes?"

"No, thank you," Matilda demurred.

"Every child needs a father, and I will try to make the best father a child could have." He took her hand in his and brushed it with his lips. "It's a promise."

Back at Retha's, Matilda closed herself into her room and bolted the door as if by doing so she could shut out the world. Her mind, like an attic, was full of a jumble of things through which she had to fight her way, things which kept falling in on her. She lay inert and hopeless with eyes closed, trying to conquer her own thoughts. She couldn't forget one statement Mr. Goldfinch had made. *Every child needs a father.* That one sentence. She must be fair to her baby no matter the anguish it caused her. If there was only some way to prepare herself, . . .

A nomad in a wilderness of frightening tomorrows, she sobbed until her face was raw from weeping. Following the bout of tears, she lapsed into a lassitude in which she seemed incapable of reasoning or action. The courage that sustained her heart had died, but her body lived on. She was too weary, too utterly dejected to rationalize.

Retha respected her need for solitude, leaving her to brood through another sleepless night.

Chapter Nineteen

The Memorial Service

April came and with it the abundance of bluebonnets.

"We'll have th' memory service for Tilly Sunday," Martha Harris told Sally on Good Friday. "Ever'body will be here by then. We can all come back t' my house for a potluck dinner afterwards."

"Sarah is making Little Henry a new suit," Sally said. "It's blue linen."

"Git out my black hat, Sally. Th' one I wore to yore Pa's funeral. The one I wore to Fort Worth when I went to see Candice's Ma."

"That old cabbage hat is outdated by two decades."

"I don't care. I'd feel plumb unclothed without it."

"Bert had an idea. He is bringing a portrait of Matilda that he painted to sit on the altar in place of a casket. That will help us all remember."

"That's thoughty of him. Git me a hankie, Sally. I can't hold back my cry."

Sunday dawned on a soft, still morning. There was a small trembling of air that wasn't quite a breeze. The golden edge of the sun swam up from the horizon with a splendor that set the eastern sky aflame as the Brazos River valley rose to a new day. Birds exchanged greetings.

"I'm thinkin' 'twas on such a day our Savior riz," Martha said. "An' 'cause He riz, we'll see our Tilly again someday on th' other side."

Sally helped Martha, slowed by age and rheumatism, to the church that filled with three generations of Harrises. A vase of spring wildflowers sat at the end of each wooden bench.

Bert took his place, holding his young son, between Hank and Sarah. His expression was drawn and anxious, his eyes brimming with a mixture of pride and sorrow. He wore his agony with dignity. The unbearable had to be borne. His mother once told him that the more one endured, the better one was able to endure. He hoped that was so, but he wasn't sure. He felt miserably alone and out of place.

If only Matilda could have lived until he finished school! He had such lovely plans for her in a brighter day with the harshness of life disbarred and only its warmth and tenderness admitted. All she had known since their marriage was a small room in a boarding-house, pinching pennies and scanty supplies. If he had known their time was so limited, he would have done things differently. He would have. . .

The service started, jerking Bert back to the present. Dessie's husband, Nathan, prayed a beautiful prayer that tightened Bert's chest. He told God what an unselfish and trusting person Matilda had been and committed her soul to His keeping.

Then Sally began to sing in her clear, soprano voice. It was a lovely melody--but, wait! Matilda had mentioned the words to him before they left home that last night. *Amazing Grace, how sweet the sound, that saved a wretch like me. . . .*

That was the song Matilda had asked him to play on the fiddle while she sang. And he had refused. He'd said his fiddle had never played hymns and didn't want to learn. Oh, if only he could relive that one afternoon! He would gladly play it for her. *Amazing Grace*. He listened raptly, finding the music touching. It haunted him now. He closed his eyes tightly, but two fierce tears spurted out.

Matthew Harris spoke of a divine reunion with Matilda in a better place, a tearless, happy setting. Bert noticed that the words comforted and relaxed Hank and Sarah, but he did not share in the assurance. He had been left out of some grand family secret.

After the service, Bert followed the crowd to the graveyard to place a wreath there for Matilda then on to Martha's for the "funeral meal" provided by the community. Dishes of all sorts lined Martha's long harvest table, sat on the sideboard, in the warming oven and even on the windowsills.

Bert had never seen so much food or such hospitality--all in honor of Matilda. She must have been a very popular young lady. He had never known the closeness of a large family; the warmth and camaraderie about him made him yearn for this unfamiliar bond. He was an only child, the son of an only child. He decided he had missed out on some special significance in life.

He said little, thought much. For the two years of their marriage, he had distanced himself from his wife's relatives. Too late, he realized his mistake. What could he have gleaned from them had he made the effort to be congenial? He had lost the precious experience of fellowship in those two years. Now, though, he was no longer a part of this family; the tie had been severed with Matilda's death. His life would move on in another sphere, and what he might have gained was forever forfeited.

All the Harrises impressed Bert, but he felt especially drawn to Martha Harris. He had been bereft of a grandmother before he was out of long gowns. Martha, with her fine, silver hair and eyes faded from the guiding of her numerous offspring from infancy to maturity, fit his mental image of a perfect grandma. Matilda had loved her grandmother devotedly, speaking often of her. Why hadn't he taken the time to become acquainted with her? She might not have minded including him under her "grandmother umbrella," too.

He would like to have one visit with the family matriarch, he concluded. Then he could pass the memory of her to his own son, who deserved a history of his roots on the Gibson side. When dinner was finished, he would watch for an opportunity to sit beside Martha for a few minutes, and they would talk. They would converse about Matilda's childhood, about the past, about anything Martha Harris wished to discuss. An eager listener he would be. Sarah would care for Little Henry while he enjoyed the discourse.

Sally settled Martha in her chair when the meal was over. Bert went to her at once, and the rest of the family, divining their need to make peace with Matilda's passing, occupied themselves with other matters.

"My Matilda really loved you, Grandmother Harris," Bert began, not knowing how to initiate the conversation.

"It was a both-way street, it was," countered Martha, dabbing at her eyes. "Tilly was always a lovin' young'un. She always had a soft conscience for doin' right. In my heart o' hearts, I couldn't b'lieve Little Tilly would ever up an' leave her husband an' baby for another man. That warn't her way. She might've growed cold t'ward church an' God after she married, but inside she was still upright."

"I am not a Christian, Mrs. Harris, but I tried not to hinder Matilda from her religion. She prayed and read her Bible a lot, and just before she left, she made a new start. The weekend before she died, she took Little Henry and went to church while I was gone to visit my mother. All that last week, she had a--a radiance."

"Well, praise be! That's heartsome news for an old an' worried grandma. I was hopin' she was soul right with God when she went out to meet Him."

"I'm sure she was."

"Why ain't you a Christian?"

"It's a long story. I was baptized into a church when I was a baby, but, of course, I don't remember anything about it. It wasn't my choice; it was my mother's, and I can't see that such a ritual could do any good. Then after my father died and I grew older, I joined a large church in an effort to fill an emptiness within. I followed the parson's instructions, but nothing changed.

"On top of this, my friend got religion at a brush arbor revival. He professed to be a real holy Joe, but indeed, religion made him a genuine hypocrite. He was worse after his conversion than before.

"So I gave up on God and decided to make a go of it in the world on my own."

"What did the parson say to do?"

"He told me to say that I believe Jesus was the Son of God."

"Jesus *is* God."

"Oh, I know that Jesus is God, the Son. The second God."

"Jesus is God th' Everything!"

"I--I haven't studied the Bible much."

"Th' knowin' who God is don't come by study. It comes by revelation. I remember th' day Tilly got her revelation. She was fourteen. It was in th' summer. She came runnin' all th' way to my house barefoot a-sayin', 'Gran'ma, look at this! Th' Bible says God is a *Spirit*. An' that Spirit was manifested in th' flesh. God was *in* Christ reconcilin' th' world to *Himself*. Did you know that, Gran'ma?' she asked. 'Did you know that th' Godhead dwelt in Christ *bodily*?'

"I told her, 'Why, honey, God showed that beautiful truth to ignerent ole me a long time ago. Read about Philip,' I said to her. 'He asked Jesus to show him th' Father, an' Jesus said, "Philip, here I am! When you see Me, you see th' Father 'cause I an' My Father are *one*!"'"

"That's interesting. I have never heard it."

"It's pure truth. An' truth is what sets us free. Why, Jesus Himself said He was th' first an' th' last. An' my Henry used to say, 'Yeah, an' ever'thing 'tween.'"

"I regret to say that I've been bitter about religion."

"Religion don't 'mount to nothin'."

"It doesn't?"

"Nope. But *salvation* does, an' there's a heap o' difference, my boy. There's many religions, an' they could all be haywire for all I know, but there's only one salvation, an' that is somethin' you git fer yerself inside yer heart. Shakin' th' parson's hand an' repeatin' a sentence won't bring salvation. I could say all day that I b'lieve I'm a millenaire, but it wouldn't make me one!"

"What is salvation?"

"It is righteousness, peace an' joy in th' Holy Ghost."

"How does one get it?"

"Jest like Tilly did. Didn't she never tell you about when she got saved?"

"She tried once, but I discouraged her from talking about God or the Bible. It made me uncomfortable because I had tried religion, and it hadn't worked for me. I didn't think the promises in the Bible were for everyone."

"Bless yore heart. I'm sorry you got sidetracked. But real salvation would help."

"Since Matilda isn't here to tell me how she got salvation, perhaps you could."

"That's my plans, young man."

Bert pulled his chair nearer so as not to miss a word.

"You know that Jesus, our Savior, died on the cross, was buried an' rose up from th' grave?"

"Yes, I know that much."

"D'ya b'lieve it?"

"Yes."

"There's yer three salvation steps. You jest follow th' Master. First you die out to old self an' his old sins. That's called repentin'. Tilly took that step when she was twelve. Then you get baptized--that equals with buryin'--in the Name of Jesus for th' erasin' of all those sins. That wipes th' slate clean but only if His Name is said 'cause that's where th' sin-takin' power is. After that, you rise up from that water grave t' walk a new life with th' Holy Ghost."

"When this happens, does one *feel* differently?"

"Absolute. An' you'll know for certain you got God's Holy Ghost gift when you speak in a different language."

"You mean, your words will be kinder?"

"No, no. You actual speak in another language b'sides English or whatever yer national tongue happens to be."

"I could never do that. I didn't take foreign languages----"

Martha held up a blue-veined hand. "'Course you can't do it, nor can me or anybody else. Tilly couldn't neither. But th' Spirit comes in an' fills yer heart, an' that's what does th' talkin' for you an' through you. It's a really live experience, an' Tilly got th' Holy Ghost in her heart when she was thirteen. She talked in a heavenly language for two straight hours. I tell you, it was th' most beautifulest sound t' these old ears o' mine, knowin' she'd been born into God's Kingdom. I can most nigh hear it yet."

"Matilda had a good heart. She was kind, lovely, godly--

everything I'm not."

"God don't go by good. None of us'ns is deservin' o' anything. It's paid for with faith. If'n you b'lieve Him t' give th' Holy Ghost to you jest 'cause He said He would, He'll do it. He'll take anybody that's a-hungerin' an' a-thirstin'--an' yore doing that right now."

"Okay, then what?"

"Live ever' day walkin' as close to Jesus as you can until He takes you on to glory to be with Tilly."

"I--I wish I could have known sooner."

"It's never too late as long as yer still a-livin' an' a-breathin'. Henry an' me was growed up an' had kids of our own b'fore we got saved. An' I was a turrible sinner, let me tell you. I was mean to a little crippled girl. God had to use lots o' scrubbin' to git this old soul clean."

"Matilda and I could have walked with God together." Regret tinted Bert's voice.

"She would've a-shouted 'bout that, but what's gone is gone, an' you gotta go on from here an' today for you an' th' little boy."

"That song Sally sang----"

"*Amazing Grace*?"

"Does she have the music to that?"

"She does. It's in our church hymnbook. It was Tilly's favorite solo, an' she could outshine Sally in th' singin' of it. I was hopin' Tilly would outlive me so's she could sing it at *my* funeral."

"Matilda asked me to play it for her on the violin, but I had never heard it, and--and----"

"Sally will be glad to give you th' notes. It has the purtiest words 'bout bein' lost an' then found an' 'bout bein' blind an' seein'. Th' second verse is 'bout grace leadin' us all home."

"Matilda told me."

"You wantin' to learn it on th' fiddle?"

"I have no violin now, but if I ever get another, I would like to play it with the hopes that Matilda could hear it in heaven. And I'd like to learn it for Little Henry since it was his mother's favorite."

"I'm feelin' that t'day is yer day of salvation, Bert. God is speakin' to yer heart. We always have family prayin' on Sunday evenin's. If you'll do some repentin', you'll be adopted into God's big family this very day, I warrant."

Bert went for a walk along the riverbank alone. He thought of all Martha had said. He was ready for a change. In fact, he could feel something beginning to happen inside now.

Chapter Twenty

The Violin

For Matilda, May slipped unnoticed into June, the prelude of a long, hot summer. Days followed other wearisome days. Time swept her relentlessly toward her destiny as despair nibbled away at her spirit like a rodent with sharp teeth. She lay down with misery, awoke to misery and walked with misery. As her body grew heavier, so did her heart. Dark shades of fatigue underlined her eyes.

Retha Bennis talked to the doctor about her. "Linda has lost the desire to live, Doctor. I am concerned about her. I fear she is grieving herself to death over the baby."

The doctor spread out his hands. "I don't know what to do for her. I thought the amnesia would be gone by now, but there has been no improvement whatsoever. If anything, she is regressing. Surely you agree that she is in no emotional condition to rear a child. You have confirmed her low mental state. It could digress even more if she suffers postpartum depression. She is a likely candidate for it. With the birth of the baby, she could lose her equilibrium completely. I am thinking of the child's best interests. Linda hasn't changed her mind about signing the adoption papers for the Goldfinches, has she?"

"No. She knows it is for the best. It's--it's just going to be terribly hard for her, Doctor."

"It is hard for any mother. She wouldn't be human if it wasn't. We will support her. Her grief will eventually pass into a fund of acceptance. Mr. Goldfinch has offered her a good job when she is able to take it. Getting away from here should contribute to her healing. At any rate, occupying her mind, getting her attention off past disappointments and on to a golden dawn can be nothing but good."

"I wish we could find something for her to do now. She sits and reads her Bible hour after hour. Reading the Bible is fine, but she needs a diversion."

"I had hoped for a miracle or, at the very least, that we might locate her family. But with every passing week, I have less hope that we will ever unravel the mystery that surrounds Linda Brown. Sometimes I'm persuaded there's sheer anarchy in the house of fate."

The "something to do" for Matilda came unexpectedly. One of the doctor's regular patients, Mrs. Keene, asked Retha if she knew of anyone who could babysit for her. Retha called a hasty conference with the doctor, and each concurred that "Miss Brown" could probably hold up to it. The doctor explained Matilda's situation to Mrs. Keene in full and left the decision to her.

Mrs. Keene was willing to take Matilda on a trial basis. She said the job would only last a few weeks; it would terminate before Matilda's confinement. Mrs. Keene's business was on the real estate market, and as soon as she found a suitable buyer and was freed from that responsibility, she would care for her small grandson herself. She had been taking him to work with her, but as he grew older and more active, she found it no longer practical or safe to keep him at the workplace.

The child was too young, she told Retha, to be affected by

a sitter's lack of morals, and as long as the girl was clean, efficient and interacted well with children, there should be no problem. She would pay the standard wage and would retain the right to dismiss the girl on questionable behavior at any time.

Matilda was pleased to find work. She smiled for the first time in many days.

Retha supplied Matilda with as many details of her new job as possible to allay her fears. Mrs. Keene owned a large trading post, where she bought and sold both new and used items. It might be furniture, tools, musical instruments, or bric-a-brac. The shop had been left to her by her late husband.

Mrs. Keene's son worked as an engineer for the Santa Fe railroad. He spent most of his time on out-of-town business. His child, James, lived with Mrs. Keene. James was scarcely out of the infant stage, still in bibs and diapers. Mrs. Keene was quite over-protective of the child. Matilda would work from eight o'clock in the morning until Mrs. Keene closed shop at five o'clock in the afternoon. Mrs. Keene would provide transportation for her.

Retha had little more information. "Your job will be to feed the child, change him and see that he has his nap. Do you think you can do that?"

"Oh, I'm sure that I can!" Matilda replied without hesitation. "I *know* I can."

Matilda watched over her charge with utmost care. She enjoyed bathing him, feeding him, and when he cried, she held him close and rocked him, humming lullabies. He called her "Inda" and clung to her skirts.

The house was a large, brownstone structure with tall south windows that caught the breeze, diluting the stifling heat. The building was encircled by a picket fence over which morning glories swarmed in a tangle of dark leaves and sleeping pods. Matilda thought if she ever had a home, she would like such a house as this. It wasn't prim and proper like the Goldfinches' imposing edifice; it held a homey welcome. She felt almost as comfortable here as she did at Retha's.

Mrs. Keene was pleased with Matilda's ministrations, but she could not contain her curiosity about the girl. Linda was neat, polite and thoughtful. Mrs. Keene could not believe that she was promiscuous.

"You don't know when your child will be born, Miss Brown?"

"No, ma'am. The doctor said early fall. I suppose that means September or so."

"And what shall you do then?"

"My baby will be placed for adoption, and I shall go to work in South Texas for a Mr. Goldfinch--unless you still need me here."

"No, I should have my business sold by then although James will miss you dreadfully. I fear he is becoming attached to you. I've never employed a better sitter."

"Thank you. I am becoming attached to him as well."

"My husband's death threw everything in my lap, you see. I managed fine until my son, Al, brought James to me. By the way, James was named for his grandpa, my father. James is such a delightful child that I want to be with him as he grows up. I had been taking him to the job with me, but I have so much junk stacked around I became concerned lest he be injured."

"I'm glad to watch him. I love children, and James is precious."

Mrs. Keene sighed, "Yes, he is. And Al is a good father, but just now he is only home for a few hours each week. This will change as soon as Al gets the timetables worked out for the railway terminals. Every child needs two parents: a father *and* a mother."

Matilda winced. Mrs. Keene was parroting the doctor.

"And of the two, a mother is more important in the early stages of a child's development. Unfortunately, James will never know his mother."

The words stung. Abby Goldfinch's mothering would be quite different from Matilda's mothering. Formal, detached, cold. Matilda would choose to hold her own baby, not relegating it to a nursemaid. Abby Goldfinch would mother only when it was convenient for her.

Matilda found herself hoping that she would have a boy to be influenced by Mr. Goldfinch instead of his wife. He seemed the warmer, the more affectionate of the two. Her baby would need lots of love.

"Is your son's wife dead?"

"Yes. She died and left him with the one child, our James."

"Couldn't he--remarry?"

Mrs. Keene frowned. "I fear that he will. He has two women pursuing him now, both modern women who are self-centered. They're interested in Al but not his child. Anyhow, no woman can take the place of one's birth mother."

Matilda restrained her tears with a great effort as Mrs. Keene continued, "I only trust that whomever Al chooses as a second wife will not mistreat James. It seems to me that substitute mothers haven't the longsuffering that God gave to natural mothers. James is my only grandson, and I could not bear to see him slighted."

"Nor could I."

As the days crawled by, Matilda found herself doing things for the child without conscious thought. It was as if somewhere at some time she had been trained in motherhood. She made toys from empty spools, barricaded doors lest he escape or hurt himself, propped pillows beside him at naptime so that he would not roll off the bed. When she towel-dried his hair, she twisted the silky strands about her finger to form soft ringlets. She blew on his stomach to make him laugh.

"She's a natural at motherhood," Mrs. Keene reported to Retha. "I see no reason why she couldn't care for her own child. James has become so attached to her that I dread the parting."

"The doctor still insists that she hasn't the emotional stability to take the responsibility of rearing a child alone. And, of course, there would be the problem of finances. The Goldfinches are quite wealthy and would be most disappointed if they did not get her child."

"If I didn't have Al and James, I would take her myself and help her keep the infant."

"You and the child have done marvels for her attitude, and I thank you for overlooking her questionable past," the nurse said.

One afternoon Mrs. Keene came home from her shop with a violin case. "Look what came in today, Linda," she said. "It is exquisite! A traveling drummer dropped it by; he had gotten it up-country somewhere." She removed the instrument from its case. "Miss Bennis told me that you play the piano well, so I thought you might wheedle some music from this fiddle."

Matilda gazed at the violin with a puzzled expression. "It--it is lovely! I don't play a violin. At least, I don't suppose I do. But it seems that I've had one like this before. I--I just can't quite remember."

"I got it at a real bargain. It would bring a pretty penny."

"Oh, please, don't sell it!" Matilda clamped her hand over her mouth, embarrassed. "Pardon me, Mrs. Keene. It is your fiddle. Do with it as you please."

"I have no intentions of selling it. I want to keep it for

James. Music runs in our family. I remember my grandfather playing the violin and how I loved it."

"I'll--I'll practice."

"Good! You may take it to Miss Bennis' with you if you'd like. I know you will take good care of it."

"Oh, yes! I will handle it most carefully."

When Matilda got home from work that day, she eagerly lifted the instrument to her chin. The bow screeched and sawed across the strings, producing an ear-abusing disharmony. Matilda was disappointed. However, she noticed that as long as she held the fiddle in her hands, she felt overwhelming peace and well-being. The serenity seemed ironic. Why should a piece of wood bring tranquility? She decided not to tell Mrs. Keene that she couldn't play it lest the woman pack it away or, worse yet, change her mind and sell it.

Matilda wanted the instrument near her at all times, but the reason was unfathomable to her. It was like an old friend--maybe even a gift from God--that had been sent to calm her fears and put her mind to rest. When torments about the past or the future crowded in, she ran for the violin and held it in her arms. The distress vanished. It didn't make sense, but it worked.

When she showed the fiddle to Retha and tried to explain the phenomenon, the nurse was baffled, too. "It may have something to do with your childhood, Linda," she guessed. "Perhaps your father or a brother or an uncle played a violin."

Retha discussed the unusual turn with the doctor. "It's amazing!" she said. "As long as the violin is within sight, Linda is placid and happy. She is like a different person. It seems the instrument serves as a sandbag to keep the waters of uncertainty at bay. It is bizarre!"

"The whole case is bizarre, Miss Bennis," the doctor said

wryly. "The Goldfinches were in today, and I told them that we certainly couldn't guarantee a normal child from such an abnormal hatchery!"

CHAPTER TWENTY-ONE

Number Forty-Two

"You say you have a prospective buyer for the business?" Al asked his mother.

"Yes. We should have the papers signed by the end of August. Then I can stay home with James."

"That's good news. I am uncomfortable with my son being placed under outside care."

"But, Al, the sitter I have hired is the very best. She loves James, and he loves her."

"That is part of the problem, Mother. James is attaching himself to a stranger. It is 'Inda' this and 'Inda' that. He jabbers about Inda all the time. He even cries for her! I don't want him accepting her as a mother figure in his life. Who is this Inda anyway?"

"She is a lady who was recommended to me by the nurse at Dr. White's hospital."

"She is an older woman, I presume?"

"No, she is just a girl."

"A girl? Left alone with my son?"

"She isn't *that* young, Al. She will soon have a child of her own. Miss Brown loves children and has a special knack with them."

"*Miss* Brown? Surely you don't mean she isn't married!"

"Well, no, not exactly. That is, not that we know of----"

"Mother! Mother!" He pounded his forehead with the heel of his hand. "Don't tell me that you've hired a tramp to care for my child!"

"Linda Brown is a very lovely girl, really, Al----"

"I don't care how lovely she *seems*, Mother. If she hasn't the proper credentials, you should never have hired her. I won't have a disreputable flapper caring for James! Didn't you insist on a background check?"

"Actually, her background is hazy. . . ."

"And she could kidnap my little boy any minute and disappear with him!"

"She wouldn't do that, Al. She plans to give up her own child for adoption to some big plum in the city's social pie. Why would she want yours?"

Al caught his breath. "Why, indeed? She may be in a ring that steals and sells children. That sort of thing is going on in our own civilized world. And some of the agents appear as angels of light, innocent, amiable, but very devious."

"Oh, Al! That thought never even crossed my mind. What you are saying is that Linda could be a wolf in sheep's clothing."

"Exactly. Linda Brown may not even be her real name."

"The doctor thinks it isn't---- Oh, I can see it all now! She pretends to be a victim of amnesia to gain the sympathy of the medical profession. When she is sure that we trust her enough, she will slip off with James----" Panic rose in her like mercury in a thermometer.

"Now you are assuming, Mother. That may or may not be the case. It likely isn't. The girl may be aboveboard, but at any rate, if my son's mother were alive, she would not approve of him being placed under the influence of anyone with low morals. Nor do I. I insist that you dismiss this girl at once. Take James back to the shop with you these last few days. Better physical danger than spiritual. If it is too much for you, I will make other arrangements for him until you are out from under the business."

"I'll keep him with me at all times from now on. My mind could never be at rest after what you have just told me. If anything should happen to our baby, I could never forgive myself. Linda Brown shall be dismissed on Monday."

Mrs. Keene had a stout speech planned for Matilda, but when James grabbed the girl about the neck and Mrs. Keene saw the pure love in Matilda's eyes for him, she weakened. In the event that the sitter was guilty of no evil, she took a softer approach.

"The shop is sold, Linda," she said, stretching the truth to its breaking point. "I won't need your help any longer. I will take over the care of my grandson myself from now on."

Matilda wilted. She had tried to brace herself for this inevitable moment, but it came sooner than she thought and unexpectedly.

"May I walk over to see James now and then?" she asked. It was almost a plea.

"No, I don't think that would be wise. James has become rather fond of you, and it would only keep his little world in an upheaval. He needs to be weaned away from you."

"I'm--I'm sorry. I was being selfish to ask." Matilda dropped her head. "And I will return your violin."

In the days that followed, James cried for "Inda," but Matilda shed tears of acute longing for both the child and the violin. Without them, the whole structure of her life rocked on the edge of disintegration. She prayed, but it seemed the wind of providence took her words, blotted them out, and shook them free of meaning.

She supposed the hard lump in her throat had become permanent; it never went away.

Her advanced size made her miserable in August's sweltering temperature. She knew that her time of delivery was near. She would like to march to eternity's Timekeeper and ask that He stop the clock, but the malignant timepiece ticked the faster, keeping time with her frightened pulse.

She ate little and slept little.

"You must eat more, Linda," urged Retha.

"Why should I eat, Miss Bennis?"

"For your health and the health of your child."

"The Goldfinches' child? They can feed it when it arrives. As for me, I am not hungry."

"What shall I do for her, Doctor?" the nurse quizzed, greatly disturbed. "She has reverted to total apathy since Mrs. Keene laid her off."

"Apathy is normal for this stage of maternity," the doctor said. "She will do little harm to the child. Nature will see to that. It is after the birth that has me worried. We could lose Miss Brown. The Goldfinches have plenty of money, and I will keep Linda in the hospital as long as is necessary, sparing nothing to restore her to health."

While the staff discussed Matilda, back in Brazos Point, Martha Harris called to Sally. "Sally, do you remember th' story o' th' girl in th' newspaper that they couldn't find a family for?"

"Yes, Mama. Number Forty-Three on your prayer list."

"Did they ever find her folks?"

"There was nothing more in the papers."

"You know what I've decided to do?"

"It won't do any good to write a letter to the newspaper and ask about her. They just printed the news item; they won't know anything."

"I know it, Sally. That wasn't even in my thinkin'. In case th' poor dear is still lost, I'm gonna move her up in Matilda's place, an' now she'll be Number Forty-Two. I'll explain to God that all my Matilda prayers are to be given to that unknown girl. God knows who she is an' who she b'longs to."

"You are determined to worry, aren't you?"

"Yes, an' I plan to worrywart God like th' widder lady worrywarted th' unjest jedge. Don't be s'prised if'n you see a piece in th' paper that says th' lost girlie has been found by her'n."

"Oh, I won't be. Anybody that can pray Bert Conner into the Kingdom of God has a talking horn straight to heaven, bypassing Central."

"Tilly planted th' seeds, an' we saw 'em sprout, I trow," Martha said. "An' speakin' of seeds, Bert brought Sarey a' Easter lily from Tilly's grave, wherever it might be, 'fore he left. Sarey is plantin' th' lily outdoors so's it can grow year by year."

"Bert will come to the reunions from now on. He said he would."

"An' in b'tween times, too. Even when he takes on a new wife, he will bring Little Henry back t' see us."

"One never knows what is inside a person, does he?"

"What really got him was th' *Amazin' Grace* song you sang."

"Because it was Matilda's favorite. He really loved Matilda. He gave her trunk back to Sarah, but he kept her Bible."

"I'm gladsome. Matilda would want her Bible in his hands. She'd be so glad he found th' Lord. Sometimes, Sally, I look way back. I wanted to crawl in th' grave with yer Pa an' die when he went. But a'body don't jest fold his hands an' stop breathin'. I reckon th' good Lord seen fit'n to keep me alive for His own reasons. Seein' Tilly's husband born again makes all th' heartache an' sufferin' seem right triflin'. An' it makes all the *worryin'* worth it."

Chapter Twenty-Two

Aware

In the middle of the night, Matilda felt the first squeeze of pain and knew what it meant. A terrible, sickening fear of the dawn pervaded her soul. Time's incessant scythe had reached her.

It would soon be over, and she was glad. What lay in her future, besides vacant arms and a heart depleted of all emotion, she did not know. The physical and mental pain meshed into one endless throb of woe.

Retha took her to the clinic, and the Goldfinches met her there for the wait. They had brought a lavish layette and a decorated basinette along with a nursemaid.

"Mr. and Mrs. Goldfinch would like for you to sign the adoption papers now, Linda," Retha explained. "Then in the unlikely event that anything should happen to you, there would be no legal repercussions."

"Couldn't I--wait?"

"The doctor thinks it would be best to get your signature beforehand."

With fingers that shook as though palsied, Matilda signed her unborn child over to the smugly smiling couple. Mr. Goldfinch licked his lips with satisfaction, and Mrs. Goldfinch's face visibly relaxed.

Matilda had been in her room for less than two hours when she whispered to the nurse, "The baby is coming."

Retha patted her arm. "It may be several hours yet, Linda. With a first child, it takes longer. Just try to inhale deeply and be brave."

But Matilda was right. Ten minutes later, the doctor held a tiny baby girl in his hands. "She is a bit underweight, but she seems as fit as a fiddle," he told Retha, who took the baby out to meet her new parents.

The Goldfinches insisted on taking "Abigail" directly home with them that day. "Absolutely not," ordered the doctor. "She will stay here until she has gained another pound. That could be a week or more. Most babies lose a few ounces after birth. Besides, early babies must have their mother's milk to avoid congestive problems."

The Goldfinches were displeased, but all their nagging didn't change the doctor's mind. They made a nuisance of themselves, hanging over the baby's crib. Abby Goldfinch seemed to fear that a dispatched death angel might slip in unawares. One or the other of them stayed at the hospital around the clock.

"I would not be surprised to find an armored guard at the door," Retha hissed to the doctor. "Tell them to go home!"

"The baby is legally theirs, and I cannot send them away," he said.

Matilda's fortitude astounded even the doctor. "I underestimated her spunk," he said.

Matilda's heart, dying within her, made the supreme sacrifice. She was doing what was best for her baby. In the deep of the night, when she held the infant to her breast, she talked to her. "You are so perfect and lovely that I cannot subject you to the deprivation and humiliation that I will suffer in my life," she said. "I love you far too much. I will never forget you, and someday you will understand that I did not forsake you nor give you up willingly. I hope that you can forgive me and someday be grateful. It is worth all my pain to know that you will not have to face the rejection that I have met."

She counted the baby's toes and fingers and caressed the small face. These moments would be filed away in her memory, for she never planned to intrude into the life of Mr. and Mrs. Goldfinch or their daughter, Abigail. She would have to trust God to help her hold no bitterness, ask no further questions.

Each day grew more difficult. The baby nestled against her contentedly. Mrs. Goldfinch watched with envy, standing ready to remove the child at the nurse's first nod. The baby often fretted and cried in Mrs. Goldfinch's arms, but with Matilda she slept peacefully.

"You'll be able to take the baby home before long," Matilda heard the doctor tell Mrs. Goldfinch on the seventh day. "She is a beautiful and healthy baby."

Those words were the shovel that dug the grave of Matilda's hopes. Without warning, something snapped within her. She tasted the salt of her tears. No! They could not take her baby! What meaning would life have without her child? Whatever the circumstances that brought the infant into her life, the child was *hers*. It didn't belong to anyone else! She would die before she would allow them to take her baby from her. They would have to pry it from her lifeless arms!

Matilda tried to reason with her unreasonable self. The papers were already signed. It was too late to change her mind. Besides, she couldn't pay the hospital bill. She had no money for clothing or blankets or diapers. But all the arguments availed nothing. The mother in her flung them all aside like so much worthless baggage. Nothing mattered but her baby. She would snatch her little girl and flee! To anywhere. She would find an abandoned shed, or they could live under a bridge. The weather was warm enough for an outdoor existence. A thrill replaced Matilda's cold nausea.

"Miss Bennis," she heard herself call. The nurse came.

"Yes, Linda?"

"How much longer will it be before the Goldfinches take the baby home from the hospital?"

"I think the doctor plans to dismiss her tomorrow." Retha smoothed Matilda's hair. "We are proud of you. You have held up well, much better than the doctor had hoped. However, we would like to keep you for a few days yet until you get adjusted to your life without the baby. Don't worry, the Goldfinches will pay for everything. Are you feeling okay?"

Matilda smiled, glad the nurse could not read her thoughts. "Thank you, Miss Bennis, I am feeling fine. You have been very kind to me."

The two a.m. feeding would be best. That was the darkest part of the night. Miss Bennis wouldn't be on duty. The doctor would be asleep. Matilda's mind made plans and counterplans. She would send the night aide for a glass of water, feigning thirst. When the aide came back, she would find an empty bed.

Excitement pinked Matilda's cheeks and brightened her eyes. The hours ran slowly and seemed to stop as the afternoon shade crawled across the ground outside the window. Matilda ate everything on her dinner tray and asked for more. Her stomach was warm around the food. She hid the extra bread beneath her pillow, making plans to stuff it in the pillowcase along with a blanket. Her heart sang.

As night came on, a full moon pried into the darkness, dusting the parking lot with silvery light. The sky burned with stars.

Matilda ached with impatience as the thought of running away with her baby roared loudly within her. How could she keep it quiet? The idea dazzled her mind like the flash of a mirror in the sun.

Calmly, deliberately, Matilda took the baby for her feeding. Then she asked the aide for a glass of drinking water, and when the aide went for the water, Matilda sprang from the bed, clutching her baby and the packed pillowcase in her arms.

Matilda's legs wobbled in a buckling motion as she moved down the hall toward the rear exit of the building. She hadn't been up for an entire week and had failed to take into consideration how weak she was from lying in bed. Her head became light, but she plunged on. Determination eclipsed her weakness. She had almost covered the distance to the door when a shrill voice rang out.

"Stop! Stop, this minute!"

Lights flashed on everywhere, and Mrs. Goldfinch came on the run, pointing and yelling. "She's trying to kidnap my baby! Stop her!" She was directly behind Matilda. "You little vixen, I knew you would try to do something like this at the last minute! That's why we stayed day and night. Bring my baby back this instant!" She sneered contumeliously as she gave a crisp snap of her fingers.

Still, Matilda struggled with the door, seeking escape. Terror pinched off her breath. She had to make it! Darkness edged in around her vision, and the top of her head seemed to lift from the lower portion, creating a diminuendo of all sound. Everything around her dwindled and blurred.

Mrs. Goldfinch reached her and tried to yank the baby from her arms, but Matilda held on with all her strength. Then the angry woman pushed her, at the same time grasping the baby by the legs.

Matilda, her balance already precarious, fell against the frame of the door and struck her head a severe blow. Her gamble had failed. A mist closed around her as she melted into the floor in a merciful miasma of unconsciousness, a soundless cry frozen on her lips against this further cruelty.

Every occupant in the hospital was awake by now. "Send for the doctor!" the aide shouted to the janitor.

"Yes, send for the doctor!" spat Mrs. Goldfinch. "I will demand that he allow me to take my child home from this hospital within the hour. I shall not chance her being kidnapped by that villain again. In fact, I will take her now." She turned to walk out.

"You will take the baby nowhere until the doctor dismisses her, ma'am," the aide said sternly. "If you do and any ill comes of it, you will be charged with first degree murder." It may have been an empty threat, but it was enough to stop Mrs. Goldfinch in her tracks.

The doctor was standing over Matilda's bed when she opened her eyes to the gray light of morning. A babble of voices hit her like pebbles. Where was she? Why was she here?

The amnesia was gone. She glanced about desperately for something familiar. Memory began as a small stream at the edge of her mind and grew with swift and terrible vitality into a tempestuous flood that ventured to drown her. "Oh, God," she prayed, "I need You."

She remembered it all. Her childhood with apple rings strung over the hearth, the smell of paraffin from the tops of Mason jars, her quilt with the State of Texas in the middle. The schoolroom, the roll call, pitched pine desks, the blackboard with its greenish cast and the schoolmarm with the chalk in her hand. Her courtship and marriage, from the drugstore to Mrs. Neuse's tiny rooms. The birth of Little Henry and the thrill of her son's first steps, his first words. The dance, the wreck. . . And she remembered sketches of the more recent hours since. Horror began to sidle into her realization. All the suffering of the past condensed into one unbearable paroxysm.

She had just given birth to Bert's baby girl, and someone was trying to take her away. She bit her lips to hold back the wild cry that filled her mouth.

"What--what day is it?" she asked the doctor.

"The tenth," he answered.

"The tenth of what?"

"September."

She calculated in her mind. She had been gone for six months, and Bert had not come for her. He thought she had left him and had run away with Pascal. Where was Pascal? She couldn't recall when and where she last saw him.

Bert would never take her back; his pride would not allow it. Bert wouldn't believe her story against Pascal's. Pascal had fooled him too many times.

Her mother would let her come home, though. Her mother would believe her. Grandmother Harris would believe her. But she had signed away the baby. Her heart sank.

Where was Little Henry? Bert would have graduated by now and moved away from Walnut Springs. That is, if he had stayed to finish his schooling. Would she ever see him again? Pascal's dirty trick must have thrown Bert into an awful quagmire.

Matilda needed time to think, time to sort things out. She wasn't willing for the doctor or the Goldfinches to know that she was cognizant of her past. Not yet. It might work against her somehow.

The doctor gave her an odd, calculating look. "Is everything all right, Miss Brown? You are shaking."

"Where is the nurse?"

"Retha?"

"Yes."

"It's early; she hasn't come in for her shift yet."

"The baby?"

"The little tug of war you and Mrs. Goldfinch had upset her. She spit up her milk. If her stomach settles, they will take her home today. That will probably be best for everyone concerned. I am disappointed in you, Linda. We all thought you were doing so well, and then you pulled a senseless stunt like this. You could have injured yourself and the Goldfinch's daughter."

"I'm--I'm sorry. I'd like to talk to Miss Bennis, please. And--and may I see the baby one last time to kiss her goodbye?"

"I will try to arrange it, Miss Brown, but the child will remain in Mrs. Goldfinch's arms, and you are not to hold her again. I hope that I can trust you."

"You can trust me, Doctor, but from now on, please call me Matilda. I'm tired of Linda."

He gave a false laugh to humor her and wrote on her chart: Psychosis, postpartum. Prognosis: Poor. Her fragile shell of sanity had burst.

Entombed in grief, Matilda cried herself to utter exhaustion and then, weak and heartsick, lost her fight to stay awake. She fell into a deep sleep.

Chapter Twenty-Three

The Fiddler's Song

Mrs. Keene awoke troubled. The sale of her business had fallen through, and James had thrown tantrums since "Inda" left. It had been three weeks, and he cried for her every day. Besides, Mrs. Keene had had a dream that nagged her.

"Al," she said as they sat at the breakfast table, "I can't get Miss Brown off my mind."

"I won't relent, Mother. A girl with loose morals will not babysit my son. Forget it."

"I believe her to be pure of body and soul, Al. I dreamed of her last night, and she was dressed in spotless white. She told me that she was innocent of any wrong and begged me to let her see James again."

"I don't know the woman. I know only what you have told me. When in doubt, I don't compromise where my only child is concerned."

"I didn't realize how much I missed Linda until she was gone. When she came, she brought her sweetness with her. When she left, I felt. . . cheated. Now I believe that she had a husband who is either dead or who divorced her. I--I almost wish you could have met her--and loved her for James' sake."

"Mother! You are out of your mind! I wouldn't consider

loving anyone simply for James' sake, much less a woman of doubtful character! I will take James away for a few days and give you a much needed rest."

"No, Al, a physical rest is not what I need. I need some answers. If you will stay with James for a couple of hours, I would like to call on Linda. I almost feel that I owe her an--an apology for ever having a bad thought about her."

"Of course, I'll stay with James. The fresh air will do you good. I've been wanting to look over the old violin. I'll do that while you are gone."

Mrs. Keene went to the nurse's house, but found that no one was there. Her intuition told her that the girl was in the hospital. Her heart sank; she wanted to talk with Linda. A conviction that the girl had been unjustly mistreated by life itself harried her. Her sense of justice cried out for the fairness that had not befallen her. She wanted to encourage Linda, tell her she understood and she believed her to be chaste and good-hearted. But Linda was gone.

Mrs. Keene returned at once, and as she opened the screen, she heard violin music coming from her son's bedroom. She tiptoed nearer to listen. Al played with precision and perfect harmony. *Just like his grandpa,* she mused. She was glad the old fiddle had found its way to her shop.

The fiddling stopped, and she heard a low sob. Should she check on James? Lost in his music, Al might not hear the child's crying. She pushed the door open gently. . . and froze.

Her son stood before the picture of a young woman, and as he played *Amazing Grace*, tears made a path down his cheeks. The glass that covered the picture had been broken and carefully repaired. Beneath the handpainted portrait were the words: "My First Love." The photo was unmistakably that of Linda Brown!

"*Al-bert!*" she raised her voice, bringing him back from

another time, another place. "Who--what?"

Her interruption was so startling that for an instant there was complete silence.

"I thought you were gone, Mother." His look accused her of trespassing. "I was playing for my wife, Matilda, her favorite song. I didn't get to play it for her before she died."

"Before she *died*?"

"I told you all about Matilda."

"Matilda was James' mother?"

"Certainly, Mother. But Matilda didn't call our son James. She called him by his second name, Henry, after her grandfather."

"If that girl in the picture is Matilda, Albert, she isn't dead."

"Pascal brought me a bowl of flowers from her grave."

"Pascal Keene may have *told* you that he got flowers from her funeral, Albert, but he didn't. Oh, that Pascal! When I married his father after the death of your own father, I tried to make a truthful boy of him, but I never did succeed. Believe me, that girl to whom you are playing is *Linda Brown*."

"Linda Brown? The baby sitter?"

"None other."

"But she would have recognized James Henry."

"No, she had amnesia. She had been in a wreck----"

"She--she was in a *wreck*?"

"Yes."

"Go on!" Bert held the bow midair.

"She remembers nothing of her past."

"And she was--was in a family way?" *The secret!* "So that was the news she had planned to whisper to me that night!"

"Unless I miss my guess, she is at the hospital right now."

Bert's hands shook. He pushed the instrument into his mother's arms. "Here! Put it in the case for me. If--if my sweetheart is alive, I will play her song to her in person. Oh, Mother! I pray that you are not mistaken."

"I am not mistaken, Albert. You have captured her so perfectly in the picture. I would recognize her anywhere. And--and everything adds up. The wreck--her love for James---- Go to her, Albert! Go, now!"

Bert needed no urging. He took the fiddle, the same fiddle he had sold to pay for his son's medicine, caught a taxi, and went forthwith to the hospital. He asked for Matilda Conner.

Miss Bennis looked blank. "She may be known to you as Linda Brown," he smiled. "She worked for my mother, Mrs. Keene."

"Oh--Linda. She is in room three, but she--she gave birth to a baby and has had a bad night."

Bert didn't wait to hear more. He pushed open the door and thought his heart would burst when he saw her, pallid and asleep but more lovely than ever, with her russet hair fanned across the white pillow. Everything he had ever felt welled up in him--the love, the tenderness, the hope--all for her, all because of her.

He quietly opened the violin case, took out the instrument, and began to play *Amazing Grace*.

Matilda thought she was having a lovely dream; she didn't want to open her eyes and find that the illusion had fled. Oh, that she could capture the fragile moment and hold it without breaking it! Was it better to remember or to forget? If she could only listen to the heavenly music on and on. . . .

She stirred restlessly then slowly opened her eyes. *Bert!* A smile stole across her blue lips. "Am--am I dreaming? Is--is it really you, Bert?"

"You remember me! Oh, my darling!" The violin was cast aside as he gathered Matilda into his arms, kissing her hair, her eyelids, her nose, her lips. "You are alive! Pascal told me that you were dead." He gave a short laugh. "We had a memorial service for you on Easter! You would have loved it!"

"I just--just today found my memory, Bert." One had to have lost and regained to know this sort of boundless joy.

"And where is our new baby?"

"I--I signed adoption papers on her a week ago. They've--they've taken her away."

"You. . . *what?*"

"The doctor convinced me that I should give her up. No one knew who I was or who her father might be, so some wealthy people adopted her."

"And doesn't a father have any rights? I didn't sign anything, and she belongs to me, too."

"Oh, Bert, they've already claimed her and named her. It's--it's too late."

"Whose name did you sign?"

"Linda Brown."

"That's not even your legal name! Those papers are not valid. No one will get my daughter!"

"Please, Bert," Matilda sobbed, "can you try to get her back for us? Can you? And where is my Little Henry?"

"You've been babysitting him, and he hasn't stopped crying for you since. But we will discuss all that after I have talked with the doctor." Bert left the room running.

Mr. and Mrs. Goldfinch had started down the hall with the Conner baby. "The nurse said I must stop by and let Miss Brown kiss the baby goodbye, but I have no intentions of doing so," said the arrogant lady. "It will only cause more problems, and I am sick of that whimpering mother. This baby is ours now."

Bert stepped in front of them. "Pardon me, sir," he said to

Mr. Goldfinch, "but you have my baby. I didn't sign the papers for her adoption, and, therefore, the adoption is not legal. If I may take her, please?"

Mrs. Goldfinch was livid. A raging fire blazed in the depths of her eyes. "Definitely not! *We* paid the medical bills, *we* furnished the clothes and blankets, *we* spent a sleepless week here caring for this baby, *we*----"

"It matters not what *we* did," Bert remained stolid. "You will be reimbursed for any expenses you have incurred, ma'am, and for your trouble, too, if you insist. I am an engineer, and the railroad has a wonderful insurance program that is more than adequate to cover whatever you have paid on my wife's bill."

"You can't just take our baby away from us, sir."

"You can't just take my baby away from me, ma'am," Bert smiled.

"*She* signed the papers."

"*She* didn't even know who she was. She had amnesia from a head injury. Her name is not Linda Brown; her name is Matilda Conner, and I am Albert Conner. I will go to court to get my baby if necessary. Matilda has a brother in Austin who is an attorney. Under the circumstances, any court in the land will be on my side regardless of your money or social standing."

Mrs. Goldfinch's face fell. "He is right, Abby," conceded Mr. Goldfinch. "You will be obliged to give up Abigail to her father."

"My condolences to you, to be sure," Bert said. "It must be a disappointment to lose your hopes for such a charming child as ours. I will pray that God, in His own time, will grant you a child of your own." He reached out and took the squirming girl, who showed signs of growing hungry, from the crestfallen woman.

Back in Matilda's room, he placed the baby into her

mother's eager arms. "She is all ours, my love," he grinned, "and Little Henry will join us shortly.

"Pascal, who was my stepbrother, is dead, a victim of his own drunkenness. I landed a good job here in Garden City when I finished school and have been living with my mother, for whom you worked. God works in mysterious ways His wonders to perform."

"Bert! You--you mentioned God!"

"Yes, darling."

"You are different."

"Everything is different. *You were lost, but now you're found; I was blind, but now I see.* Thanks to God's *Amazing Grace* and Martha Harris' amazing prayers."

Bert encircled them both in his arms, arms that Matilda knew would hold her world together forever. The impatient baby noisily smacked at her fist. "What will we name our daughter, my first love?" he asked.

"How about Martha?"

"Perfect! Henry and Martha. Just wait until your grandmother hears about this chapter of her life!"

"The world can't do without a Martha to worry," Matilda's bubbling laughter filled the room.

Against Matilda's shoulder, the new Martha gave a hungry grunt. "She seems to be worrying about food now," chuckled Bert. "But I think her mother can do something for her."

"And her father can do something for her mother," teased Matilda.

"Anything, my first love."

"Play the violin again, Bert, while I feed your daughter. Play my favorite song."

Never had Bert played with more fervor, more feeling. The notes swelled and rose, reaching into the hall, out into the street.

The Fiddler's Song

The doctor ceased his writing, the nurse stopped in her tracks, the birds hushed their twitterings. It seemed the whole world paused to listen to *The Fiddler's Song*.